The Cursed Temple

by Gaurav Choudhury

This is a work of fiction. Similarities to real people, places, or events are entirely coincidental.

THE CURSED TEMPLE

First edition. February 11, 2024.

ISBN: 979-8224950591

Written by Gaurav Choudhury.

Table of Contents

Synopsis

A doctor illustrates story of his life. In youth, he had adventurous spirit and ended up in an expedition to India. He travelled to various parts in India and then found a man who aided in fulfilling his lust for adventure. He then illustrates tale behind the Cursed Temple, his journey to it and encounter with a demon. Finally he ends up illustrating the most surprising part of his expedition.

The Beginning

Last rays from the Sun flooded my drawing room. It looked so lovely and enchanting. Far away the flowing river Thames looked even more charming. The Sun's rays penetrating deep within the river water looked like floating with the river waves, waves in turn appeared as golden ribbon, a view as if gifted to Earth from heaven. At this age and stage of life, when a man gives up all hopes to live, these scenic beauties give an inspiration to live and rise up with new hopes. Whenever I come across this captivating beauty of the nature, I feel an inspiration and new energy build up within my heart. The Sun's rays make me merry and cheerful, gives me hope that there is still something in this world on which I can live upon. But alas!

Human beings are perishable.

In ever changing life, only death is inevitable!

There have been little showers of rain few hours ago and the sky looked clear apart from few groups of dark clouds. I stood near window at my study room, enjoying the beauty of the nature while unknowingly time had trickled quite a bit. It was possibly about an hour that I was standing by the window. I have been feeling quite uneasy for past few days. I'm growing older and feebler day by day now. After a while I looked back to my study room and at the pile of papers lying on my desk. Today is Sunday and it's a day off for me, so there was no patient. Patients, huh! Well let me introduce myself. I'm Dr John Robert Morrison, a general physician by qualification and profession. My desire or rather lust for adventure, tourism and exploration did not take me through a long and good medical career. After obtaining my primary medical degree I retired from my academic career.

I'm still single, live in a two bedded-room, fairly furnished apartment and own a private chamber down the street. I had no plans for today, I never work on Sundays. I'm 72 years old now and my lust for life and exploration has almost died. There was a time in my life when I was least bothered about life and death but then something happened and my thoughts had changed drastically. I had numerous experiences throughout my life; some have been sweet memories to cherish while some were deadly. From past few days I was wondering if I could write something from my old days, some deadly experiences which had stunned me and still remain enigmatic. Frankly speaking I'm not an author and not at all ashamed to confess that I never wrote a single page in my life! However, I was thinking from past few days to write some stunning experiences that I had in my old days and so I've picked up a pen to describe that tale of my life, which I had concealed from everyone till today. A tale which remains an enigma to me till date and it might be possible that I'll never be able to understand what exactly happened. It had haunted me through several nights initially; sometimes I felt extremely scared and woke up several times in the night, feared that someone might be watching me. However, with time I had learned to adapt, live and carry on but still sometimes those memories haunt me as nightmare.

Chapter 1

Before illustrating the series of events I encountered, it will be judicious enough to give a brief background of myself. I'm a British by birth, born and brought up in London. I completed my first class primary Medical degree from King's College, London and then declared an end to my academic career. I never had any goal for higher study and medical degree was solely based on my father's wish. In my youth I was imprudent and did not care for my own well-being. Standing just over six-feet tall, I was then strongly build, with brown eyes, flattened brown hairs and oval shaped face, more elongated towards the bottom. I always wanted to try different things and explore new avenues of life and the world. As a result, I had no fixed goal and never settled in one place or one job. After completing my medical degree, I initially tried to practice in a few private chambers but did not quite meet with good luck. Then I joined a hospital in London which again I gave up after few months of service. The superintendent was quite angry with my short term service. He gently expressed concerns that the patients I treated might be impacted with this sudden movement. I was determined and did not listen to him. Changing jobs frequently had become a routine for me by then.

I was not famous among my friends either; frankly speaking I had very few friends. I always remained confused; barely able to decide what I should do in my life or rather what should be the goal of my life. My father called me 'Johnny' and my friends were pleased to use that name while others called me Robert Jr after my father Dr Robert Morrison. It was my father's wish to study medicine and become a physician. I was more inclined towards learning philosophy or anthropology. I could not explain him what was the aim of my life. Finally, my desire to study philosophy or anthropology could not outsmart my father's decision and so I obeyed whatever he directed or decided. My father expired when I was 20 years old. He was himself a renowned physician at the East End and left me quite a fortune, sufficient enough for the rest of my life to survive without doing any job. Few years later, my mother departed too, when I was a medical student. Since, I was their only child, I became alone. With the help of a distant maternal Aunt and Uncle, I arranged my scattered life at that time and organized requirements. I had to complete the funeral of my mother within a short span of time and went back to my medical school to continue my studies. It took some time for me to recover. I'm not an emotional type of lad from heart but at my mother's funeral I wept a lot for the first time in my life. Life looked empty and hollow without her. I remembered her last words. She always wanted me to be happy and more careful about whatever decisions I took in my life. At her death bed, she kissed my cheeks for the last time and whispered in my ears "My dearest, it's my end! I can see the gates to heaven open for me, or maybe I'm wrong, it's the hell. Whatever be it, my only regret is that I have to leave you at such a young age. Try to be more careful in your life and avoid doing nasty things! May God be with you my love!" Those were her last words and I should've have followed those, instead of running after my obsession. Had I followed my mother, I might have a different life today; may be a happy family life and a reputed medical career similar to that of my father. But I chose to pursue my obsession.

From my school days I had a relentless desire towards adventure and exploration. I used to dream that when I'll grow up, I'll save lots and lots of money and set to journey to visit different parts of the globe. For a single moment in those days I had not given a thought to pursue a good career, job, house, family, etc. These were something for which I have been least bothered for my entire life. After leaving the medical school, whatever be the job or means of earning, within a few years I saved sufficient capital and added with fortune left behind from my father, I was ready to fulfill my dream to explore the world. I was not sure where to start from, thinking every day about one destination and changed it the very next day. I had a long unseen life ahead of me, with no one beside me. No one to live for, no one to die for, no one to guide and no one to warn!

For few weeks I had joined a club of amateurs and enthusiasts towards adventures and sordid journeys. Few renowned people in that club boasted about their adventures and falsified stories about their perilous journeys. Stories encompassing weird creatures, unseen or unheard realms, which were nice to hear but ultimately turns out to be mere stories. I got bored day by day and finally one day I decided to move out. Nobody seemed bothered when I moved out or expressed any concern. I felt as if this was a good escape.

When I was a kid, I heard that my father had an elder brother. I heard he was in the Royal English army and was posted somewhere in India. He was also unmarried like me. I never saw him in my childhood and rarely heard from him. I had only known him through his photos and his letters which were scarcely written. I also came to know that he was good in cricket. From what I had heard, he was heavily built and taller than me. He joined English army, fought for the country, then got promoted and transferred to India. After being transferred to India, he used to send few letters to my father initially. The frequency of the letters was very less. After my father's death letters practically stopped from him, except now and then and a Christmas greeting.

One cold evening in October 1936, I was sitting idle at a road side cafeteria sipping from a cup of coffee and considering on my next plans. I lazily sipped through my cup of coffee bit by bit and engrossed in deep confused thoughts. Absolutely ignorant about my future, I was then thinking on an expedition to South America. Starting from Brazilian Amazon forests, I thought on a plan to explore still southwards to South America, somewhere towards Chile or Peru. Also at the same time, I was thinking if I could practice medicine in Brazil for a while, so that my medical knowledge will not die and also I'll come to know more about local people and culture. It won't be difficult practicing medicine in Brazil. I had a childhood friend who had moved to Brazil

2 years ago. I was well connected to him via letter. He moved and started practicing in Brazil and was well established by now. He was married and had a family now. We had been in the same school and college and were deeply connected to each other, although my fickle mind did not match up with his. He was family oriented and was even scared to think of such lustrous and adventurous explorations. He would definitely not support my ideas but on the other hand will not deny putting forward a helping hand. The only thing that I needed now was a strong determination and a final consent from the bottom of my heart. As I had already described that I practically had no family, it was not difficult for me take such an audacious decision. But, Holy Christ! If only I had slightest idea about what was coming to me! My father used to say "Johnny boy! A man makes his own fate and not fate makes a man!" I had always believed his saying until when situations took a different direction for me. I still feel that I had disappointed my father, not been able to become someone who he always had dreamt off. Sorry father, I hope you'll forgive me!

As far as I can remember, it was Sunday and there was a little rainfall earlier that day. The streets and footpaths were wet, not to mention a cold and humid weather that prevailed. The cafeteria was warm and did not attract much of evening customers possibly due to rain. So a vacancy and calm environment prevailed. In short this was good enough for me to take final decision. I was deeply lost in my own thoughts, thinking on my plans for Brazil and South America while occasionally observing a recently received letter from my now Brazilian friend and a map of South America, when a strong hand shook my shoulder. Surprised a little bit, I glanced over my shoulder. Beside me stood a massively built masculine figure in his late sixties, grinning at me. At first I didn't recognise who the gentleman was, shortly after that I realised it was none other than my Uncle Albert Morrison, the man I had only seen in pictures and heard about till date. The only differences from the pictures were that he has grown significantly old, he had white hairs and beard and also had put on some weight, a belly protruding out giving signal about his current stature. His skin had become sun tanned, which you would normally see when exposed to too much of sunlight quite for some time. This was the first time I was seeing him in my life in person. My mother had told that he had visited us once or twice when I was small but I could not recall those times. To maintain etiquettes, I rose up from my chair and produced my right hand forwards with an anticipation of a strong hand shake. Instead my Uncle took me in his arms. I was a like a baby in his arms. Settling down in a chair next to me, he asked about my well-being and current life, career, etc. I gave a brief overview of my family incidents and my current situation, well concealing my future plans.

Uncle shook his head in grief. He was silent for a while. Then he started.

"I was away for a long time, had no connection with my family. I heard about Robbie's loss but did not know about your mother's demise. I'm sorry! Your mother was an angel. You should be proud of her". Indeed I was proud of her. Her love, affection, caring and her contribution to my life cannot be written in words. Uncle started again.

-"So what are your next plans now?"

-I replied "Haven't quite thought about it. Just considering on the idea of relocating to Brazil. I've a childhood friend over there, who is a physician as well. He is well established and can help me to get things together."

-Uncle now looked at the map lying on the table and was pretty much surprised. I had forgotten to hide it! "Why Brazil? Is it just only a career plan to settle there or you've something else going around in your mind? You can settle here in London."

-I hesitated a bit. He continued, "You can tell me, maybe I can give you some generous suggestion, although I've not been quite in touch with your family or you."

It was then I detailed him about my plans. There was no point behind hiding it. He looked all good to me and also I had made a mistake to keep the map lying on the table in front of his eyes. He stayed quite for a while. Then without any expression he started, "Young man, I will not suggest you on your decision but from my life's experience I can warn you about the consequences."

-He went on "This is no joke, I have been the same in my youth. I travelled to different parts of the world and then was in India for some time. I have no family, no one to look after and no one to care for me, absolutely no family responsibility. In youth you might have lot of ecstatic visions, which may look charming but believe me, with age you might repent."

-"I'm determined. Like you, I also have no family. Just going on."

-He shrugged and continued, "Well then, no more comments on this. But why Brazil, have you thought about any other region."

-"Like where?"

-"Why not India? India is like a dreamland! So many cultures to explore, such a great geographical diversity, which you'll find no where on Earth. It will be an expedition to remember." Alas, truly it was memorable, to be precise the experience was a nightmare and haunted my dreams for a long time. He went on, "There are so many places to visit, so many things to explore, a myriad of possibilities or even more. At one extreme, towards north there are Himalayan ranges while at other end in the extreme south you'll find Indian Ocean. There are forests, hilly regions, sea beaches, gardens, forts, palaces, temples, churches and lots more. Also, I haven't seen so much diversity in religion anywhere in the world."

-I said, "I'm not familiar with anyone in India. Where should I start from?"

-"I've few references, they can help you out. Just let me know when you are ready to sail."

-I was excited, "As soon as possible, either by the end of this month or the beginning of next month. I will equip myself with some amenities and finance and then I'm ready. It will take few weeks of time."

-"Very well!" Uncle took out a small notebook from his pocket and jotted down few names and details and gave it to me. He then rose up from his seat. "I'll be in touch with you for about a week. I was promoted to Colonel last year and transferred to United States. I stalled my transfer because I wanted pay a visit to you and your mother. But then, I'm sorry! Next week I'll be leaving for United States. Possibly this will be my last journey. I'll need to settle down there. I'm old and much feeble now. Possibly my last days have come."

-I exclaimed "Last days!"

-Uncle grinned a little, "I'm suffering from lung cancer."

I was expressionless for a while. I won't say it was not concerning me but I wasn't emotional. "Can I ask you a question?"

-He looked inquisitively at my eyes, "Go ahead, clear your mind. You should not have any doubts. Doubts will keep on troubling you."

-"Why did you leave the family, did not keep any connection with us? Was there any reason?"

Uncle seemed to be serious. His smile went away. He looked out at the street for a while as if searching for something. Calmly he said, "You know", he paused a little, looked a bit melancholy as if when someone loses great moments of life and then went on "there are some things in life that cannot be expressed. In my youth I had an imprudent nature. I did not have any structured career plan. I had not lived up to my father's expectations. I was more dedicated to serve my country and countrymen. A fickle mind describes me better. Sometimes I could not take a decision and often when I took a decision, it turned out to be disastrous. I had a quarrel with my father and then departed from home, promising never to return. Also, with my kind of nature, it was better for you all that I stayed away from the family, so that I cannot be a pain to my near and dear ones."

He then looked straightly at me and said, "I'll advice you to reconsider your plans. You may not understand the importance of family at this moment but I wish you do not live my life."

He rose on his feet, grinned a little again and then headed towards the street.

Chapter 2

I sat back still for a while trying to recall the entire discussion between me and my Uncle. I was bit confused. Few minutes later, I relaxed my chin on my folded palm over the coffee table and glanced at the South American map lying on the table. So India! I never expected, at least till today this name was almost beyond my imagination. After few thoughts, plus and minus of benefits and damages, finally, I made up my mind, closed the map, rose up from the seat, paid the bill and headed towards a book stall opposite to the street to begin my exploration.

Next few weeks were terribly busy for me. I had purchased few books on India and Indian people. This was the only way I can research on the enigmatic land where I wished to visit. In these few weeks I gained good amount of knowledge about India. The more I turned over the pages, it turned out to be more fascinating. I learned about regions, religions, about people, food habits and lots more. Meanwhile, my Uncle had visited me thrice, dropped a letter to his Indian colleague about my arrival. He also suggested me to purchase a few essential commodities that will come handy. He repeatedly warned me about mosquitoes. Two weeks after we met at the cafeteria, he left for United States. I paid a visit to him at the airport. He hugged me for the last time and departed.

While I was getting prepared for my journey, one event, even though not so much worthwhile to note at that time but I later felt was connected to my travel and life somehow. At that time, I used to practice at a local chamber at East End. One evening, few days after my Uncle had left for United States, I received a call from a patient's family. This patient was new to me. He resided in an apartment somewhere in the West End as far I can remember now. That evening, I was monitoring a recently recovered patient when I received a call from this patient's family member. I heard a female voice over the phone.

She mentioned the patient to be terribly sick and requested my urgent visit. She described a few signs but could not give an exact picture of his illness. She provided me the address and informed that the patient wished to see me at his apartment. I was not sure from where she received my contact details and also I did not remember to ask. Before I could ask for some more details on the patient's condition, she hung up. As I had no further plans for that evening and did not have any other patient in my chamber to examine, I decided to visit.

This part of the city was not so much crowded and it was not difficult to find his building and the apartment where the patient resided. The building was quite old and so was the flat. He lived in 2nd floor. I knocked on the door, waited for a while anticipating response and knocked again. After knocking 2-3 times, the door opened with a slight creaking sound. A young girl possibly within 20 years of age stood behind the door. Her voice was very soft and low. She looked tensed and scared. She asked me if I was the doctor on call. I replied yes. Possibly she was the patient's daughter. She let me in and led me to the bedroom where the patient was. While passing through the drawing room towards the bedroom I had a quick look of the room. The apartment was small, it had may be two or three rooms at the most and was averagely furnished. Sign of poverty was evident! I had a strange feeling when I entered the apartment. I saw a book-shelf full of books on astrology, occult and similar topics. There were strange looking items spread all over the room. Wall hangings consisted of strange shapes and structures as well as some demonic looking pictures. Most of the items I've never seen. I recognized Tarot cards and Ouija board which I had seen in books but others were new to me. I wondered what could be the profession of the patient or rather how the family made a living.

The bedroom was smaller than the drawing room. When I entered the bedroom, I felt a strange pungent odor. It made me almost sick. The room was dark and initially I could not see through it. Few minutes later my eyes were able to adjust to the darkness and then I saw a faint beam of light coming from one corner of the bedroom. Also, I got adjusted to the pungent odor. There was a small bed located at the left corner and it was so small that only sufficient enough to barely accommodate two people at a time. The patient was lying on one side of the bed. He was in mid 50s, thin, had untidy face due to not shaving for quite some time and looked very weak. His hairs were grayish; he had wrinkles all over his face and a small scar on the right cheek. I asked about his illnesses in details. His voice was feeble and he looked tired. I got a strange freaky feeling looking at his eyes, they resembled that of a dead fish! His entire body was covered with a shabby old blanket. I asked to produce his hand so that I can feel his pulse. As I felt his pulse, a chilling and shocking sensation went down through my spine. I was quite surprised to find that the hand was stone cold, similar what one can feel in a dead body. I performed some quick routine checks and gave some primary medications to the patient. I was not able to conclude what was the exact problem in the patient. It was somewhat like hitting around the bush. While I was performing my routine checks, the girl brought me a cup of coffee. While having my coffee, for the first time I took a closer and detailed look on the girl. She was young and very thin, had golden or brown hairs, I don't exactly remember. Her complexion was milky white and her eyes were green. She had no resemblance to the patient. I wondered how she was related to the patient. After having my coffee I wrote down a prescription slip, jotted down some points and explained those both to the patient and the girl. The girl listened to each detail very patiently but made no comment. I also suggested them to visit nearby hospital for further tests and treatment if these medicines and prescription did not help. With this I ended my session and rose up to my feet. As I took my fees and made a move to head towards the door, the man suddenly grabbed my right arm by the elbow and stopped me. I again felt the same chilling and shocking sensation and was quite surprised due to this behavior.

He whispered in my ears, "You are in great danger, stars are not in your favor. Be careful, something wicked is waiting for you." I was shocked, stared at him for a while and asked him about it but he remained silent. I asked him again but he remained motionless. Puzzled, somewhat thinking whether I heard him correctly, I slowly headed towards the entrance. When I reached the entrance I turned back to the girl. Lot of questions were hovering my mind, I needed an answer. I was filled with doubt and anxious to know about the questions.

I asked her, "Your father, I mean the person on the bed whom I met, is he a fortune teller or something similar?" I couldn't think anything better to ask.

Girl stared at me for a while and responded softly "Yes".

I gathered some stability of my mind and reframed my thoughts, "How did he come to know details about my danger, I mean he stated I was in great danger. So, how did he find that? What he told me is quite confusing. What danger he was referring to, I mean you can understand, I need to know more details on this."

The girl was silent for a while, then replied, "He has some special abilities. When someone is in danger, he can sense that in advance".

I reluctantly stepped out of the apartment and asked again, not feeling any relief from what the patient warned me, "So, your father, how long he has been practicing this, whatever it is astrology, occult or fortune teller? What danger did he see for me?" The girl almost immediately replied, "Cannot tell about your danger. He is into this profession for a long time, even before I came to his life". She paused for a while and then continued, "he is not my father, he is my husband". She did not say anything else and almost slammed the door over my face. I felt overwhelmed, confused and headed towards the street. Dreadful thoughts kept lingering in my mind. That night I could not sleep for long hours, thought about this visit and sequence of events again and again. Particularly what disturbed me was the astrologer's warning. What danger, when it is going to happen, how would I come to know about it and lot of other questions kept on troubling me but I did not find any solution. Two days later I came to know the astrologer, I could not think of a better word to describe him, had expired on the next morning of the day of my visit. I had a sudden uneasy feeling in my heart and remembered that chilling and shocking sensation. I never again visited that apartment.

I overcame the incidence which happened on that evening and it almost volatilized from my mind. Also, I was very busy in packing my luggage, so I practically did not get any time to concentrate on the incidence. One fine morning in early November 1936, I boarded on a flight to India. I had three huge bags equipped with different items. There were clothes, grooming items, books, some preliminary medicines and medical products and lots more. I also took a small bag carrying some important documents.

Chapter 3

India! A Dreamland, a magical country! At extreme north the Great Himalayas stand as guards. On three sides covered with 3 vast water bodies: Bay of Bengal, Arabian Sea and the Indian Ocean. Enormous diversity in culture, religion, food habits, clothing, ceremonies and lots more. I'll not waste time describing all these and quickly get into the main content. After travelling and visiting different places for over 1 month I finally landed into Calcutta, the former British capital of India. I had obtained few contacts in Calcutta from my Uncle. With the help of one of the contacts I rented a small apartment near College Street and planned to halt my journey and take rest for few days. I was having a difficult time to adjust to India's weather. Also, there were plenty of mosquitoes. Over 1 month I had visited different places in India and was practically tired to take more trips, temporarily. I had continuously travelled throughout this 1 month and never rested for even a single day. Moreover, there was something in Indian climate that resulted in a lot of exhaustion, although it was January 1937, still the mid-hours of the day and afternoon were comparatively warmer compared to the weather I had experienced in London throughout my life before visiting India. Calcutta also had a humid climate which contributed in further exhaustion. Over the past month my food habit has changed. The meals mostly consisted of rice, chapatti and vegetables with partly non-veg add-ups. In Calcutta I came across a lot of sweets. It appeared like the sweet hub of India. Varieties of sweets ranging from soft consistency to hard, sometimes scented, all were delicious and quite enjoyable.

Mosquitoes had been quite a concern throughout my journey. I was careful enough not to be bitten by mosquito but still could not prevent it much. Thankfully I did not get malaria or any other mosquito-borne disease. Wherever I went, I searched or requested for mosquito curtains, the best way to escape mosquito invasion.

Within few days I became familiar with the place, people and environment and also learnt some of the local language, Bengali. Also, I came to know about a club for adventure enthusiasts like me and within few days made my way towards the club. Within last few weeks I also had developed a habit of smoking, however, it was minor, nothing serious. One fine Friday evening towards the end of January 1937, after spending a bouring morning, I was relaxing on a couch at the club, in a half inclined position and reading a medical journal article on immune disorders which I had brought along with me from London but did not yet get a chance to have a look at it. I had arrived at the club earlier, in the late afternoon, and decided to hang around for a while. Since, I was new to the club, so I was still pending to build a friendly relationship. As I was not quite good at making friends, I did not find any luck at the club and was almost lonely, except few "Hi" and "Hello". While resting at the couch, I came across some familiar faces which I had seen over last couple of days, greeted them and in return they exchanged greetings. That was all, no conversations, no jokes, nothing! I lazily glanced at the journal, without any attempt to read, holding a half-burnt cigar between my fingers in the left hand which I had smoked bit by bit over past 2-3 days. I felt as if I was wasting my time at the club and thinking over last few days to travel towards north Eastern region of India.

It was late evening hours then, probably after 8 PM and the club was practically vacant. The portion of the club where I was relaxing, was totally empty and dimly lit compared to the rest of the club hall. I had known some native Bengali people who helped me to get settled here for a while, idea being to rest for few days and then to decide about further travel plans. The dinner was usually served at my apartment late at around 9:30-10:00 PM and so I had plenty of time to retire back to my apartment. I was not able to concentrate on the article and in between reading the article every now and then my eyes were hovering throughout the hall with an anticipation to find someone to speak to.

Suddenly a new face appeared in front of me from nowhere out of the dark. It was so sudden that it put me into a shock. If I remember, I did not see the person approaching towards me, it was like the person had suddenly evolved in dark from nowhere. It was a short, masculine figure. As the person stood in front of me, I immediately lifted my eyes and tried to take a thorough notice on the newly arrived stranger. As already mentioned, this part of the hall was darker compared to other parts, so I could not make out well out of the unknown figure that stood in front of me. From what I could comprehend, he looked like a middle aged man, short heighted, round faced, bald headed and somewhat obese. He appeared to have a small black mole on the chin. His skin was tanned in India's weather which made it hard to recognize if he was an Indian or of British origin.

He produced his right hand towards me and shook hands with me. Amusingly his palm was quite soft for a man and was very cold. He said, "Hi, I'm Christopher Davis. You seem to be new here. I come to this club now and then but haven't seen you before. I live here in Calcutta." I offered him a cigar.

I was happy to find someone to speak to, "Yes, I'm new. I came to India last month and shifted to Calcutta very recently. I'm John Morrison. I happen to be a doctor."

I lit his cigar and he started: "Interesting! So what brings you here?"

I did not want to give details at first, so briefly said, "Nothing special. Just a sort of a tour, visit places, have some nice food and that's all."

He frowned a little bit, "What are you doing in Calcutta? There aren't many places where you can visit in Calcutta."

I felt it was bit difficult now to conceal my adventurous purpose. I still said, "I tripped for more than 1 month and thought to take a break and rest for a while."

He quickly pulled a chair and got seated in front of me. He continued, "I see. If you like visiting places, then I can suggest you some places in Bengal. I had been in Bengal quite for some time, fell in love with this land and Calcutta and so decided to settle here."

I: "Do you have a family?"

He: "Yes, I stay at the Southern part of this city. At my home there are only two of us, my wife and myself. I have two daughters; both of them are married and settled in England, one at Berkshire and the other one at Bristol. They occasionally visit India."

I: "What did you find so interesting that you've settled here?"

He: "I'm now 62 years old. I came to India when I was only 22 years old. I took a job in the railways, something related to railway tracks and all that stuff. I had been to different parts of India. This country has a great influence on me, particularly Bengal. This land has become inherently attached to my heart and mind. So I decided to settle here and spent the last years of my life."

I: "I can see you deeply love this land. So, what drove you to select Calcutta?"

He: "Last 25 years I've stayed in Bengal and visited different parts of it. I love the culture, food, art, especially villages."

I frowned a bit and asked: "Villages? What's so special about them?"

He: "Villages and the people inhabiting them are very simple, poor but friendly. Fresh air in villages brings peace to heart and soul. If you spend some time in the village, I'm sure you'll fall in love too! The rural part of Bengal has traditional art and culture and this is quite impressive. However, you need to have a knack towards art to understand it well." He went on describing salient features of villages and the villagers by way of emphasizing his different visits to Bengal's villages and his life's experiences with them. I won't say I was not impressed by Christopher's tales but I was hoping to find something exciting that actually compelled me to travel such long distance to

India. After all, my only aim was not just a trip or long term tour but some kind of exploration that will remain memorable. I was not much interested in art, music or orthodox life style. What I was looking for was something unusual and completely apart from what normal humans think. This is bit hard to explain. In fact, I myself was not sure what I was looking for. In my childhood, my mom used to tell me several bed time stories comprising of adventures and fairy tales. This had an immense impact on me and as I grew up, my interest towards adventures and explorations kept on increasing. Over 1 month I had visited different parts of India and often found people delivering different stories out of their bucket of overwhelming nature, which at the end of day turned out to be mere exaggerating false tales. Sometimes these tales impressed me but when I tried to drill down further I was disappointed each time. Villages were something which never crossed my mind till date.

I was smoking and listening to Christopher with full attention. Suddenly, he mentioned something which interested me. I asked again, "what did you say, Cursed Temple?"

He stopped and tried to hide something from me: "It's nothing, just a traditional belief which the villagers had about it."

I: "can you tell me some more about it, this seems something interesting."

For some unknown reason he tried to avoid. Christopher looked pretty scared about something. He said, "it's nothing, just a slip of the tongue. Don't bother." Before he could proceed further a nearby clock buzzed with a loud sound alarming that it was 10:00 PM. I was startled. I was so deeply immersed in Christopher's tales that I could not keep track of the time.

I asked: "I want to listen to that part of your experience."

He shivered a bit and repeated: "It's nothing, just a slip of my tongue. Nothing was actually there. It's late today, I must leave. My wife is alone at home." Saying this he stood up, lit out the cigar and dumped it in a nearby garbage can.

I resisted: "I want to know about it. I've been in search for something interesting."

He behaved strangely: "it's better if you ignore it. Request you to visit my residence tomorrow evening for a dinner. You are cordially invited. My wife and I shall be very glad to have you for the evening. After all not many people come to my home, especially someone from my home country. I'll tell you stories of my village experiences and also show you some pictures of my visit from my album. I bet you'll like them. This is my residential address." He gave me a card carrying his name and residential address.

I was not going to give up and insisted about the Cursed Temple tale. Christopher kept on refusing, giving some pretext, however he ultimately agreed to tell that story of his visit. Before he left he warned me, this is something that I should ignore and should never think about. I just replied that I'll think about it but gave no consent. If only I had known then, how disastrous this could be!

Chapter 4

Shortly after my meeting with Christopher I returned to my apartment. It was late at around 10:30 PM. The streets were already vacant except for few stray dogs. The building where I had rented the apartment was located on a narrow lane. My apartment was located in the first floor. I had no hurry. A maid servant used to clean my apartment in the morning while a male cook prepared some food for my lunch and dinner in the afternoon. Apartment was shabby as like the building and the entire locality, where the building was situated. It had 2 rooms, 1 bathroom and 1 kitchen. The rooms were averagely furnished, minimal furniture just to suffice day to day needs. Wherever I had travelled in India, I had to stay in shabby places mostly, with only a few instances of luxurious stay. Although, the places were shabby, they satisfied basic requirements sufficient enough for at least a few days. The apartment in Calcutta was no better; however, only difference was that I was going to stay here at least for a while. I went to the bathroom directly to wash my face and freshen up. Next, I quickly completed my dinner and post dinner occupied the chair and table near to the only window of the apartment. Over past few weeks I also had developed a habit of writing down my experiences in a note book, day wise. Last few days were uninteresting and there was nothing to write. I filled the note book whenever I encountered something interesting. The meeting with Christopher that evening was flashing my mind and I could not think of anything else other than the two words "Cursed Temple". As I sat back at my chair thinking about events of that evening, it suddenly occurred to me the card which carried Christopher's residential address was left at my desk but I could not find it. I started searching for the card. I searched for it all through the room, checked my coat's pockets and all other places but could not see the card. Nevertheless, I had memorized the address. It looked bit odd to me, I did remember to leave the card on my desk before having my dinner. I clearly remember the card was still with me when I came inside my apartment, I did not lose it. At that point of time I had thought that I might have misplaced the card somehow but now when I think over it again and again it looks like it was rather something else. Later that night I did not have proper sleep. I kept on thinking about Christopher and the conversation. I felt something uneasy going down my throat, not sure what it was. I remembered the warning from the astrologer, which had almost volatilized from my mind and then this meeting with Christopher. Were these interrelated? Was I truly in some kind of danger? These questions kept on hovering my mind but there was no solution.

Next evening at around half past six, I visited Christopher's residence. It was already dark by then. His residence was located in the southern part of Calcutta then. Strangely, the area where his house was located was quite lonely. There were no street lights in the area and I found it hard to move through the darkness. Luckily I carried a small torch in the breast pocket of my coat. I used this small torch for purpose of examining my patients. Although the torch dimly lit the streets, I was still able to make out my way through the darkness. There did not seem to be any locality within 1 mile of his residence. Probably Christopher preferred silence and peace. The house was quite sober. I remembered to pass by a small pond and a group of coconut trees before his house. These might prove to be useful landmarks in case I visited this place I future. The coconut trees in the darkness displayed a ghostly appearance. Christopher had a build up a two-storeyed house. The entrance to his house consisted of a gate built from solid iron bars which carried some engravings made of brass. Beyond the gate there was a small garden. Sweet smells from some unknown flowers stroke my nose. I could not identify which flowers they were, although it is worth to mention that I was not at all good at recognizing plants or flowers. Inside Christopher's house I found quite a luxury. House was well furnished with expensive furniture sets. Walls were expensively painted and richly decorated. There were different wall hangings both oriental and occidental styles. Also there were plenty traditional items of art. The rooms were spacious, well illuminated by expensive chandeliers. When I entered the house I could smell a sweet fragrance and this prevailed all the time I stayed inside the house. I was elated. Christopher greeted me with a warm smile and welcome. I had purchased a packet of Bengali sweets for the couple as these were most common in Calcutta and a bottle of good wine. This was the best I could find in the market. Christopher's wife appeared to be almost of her husband's age but still retained beauty at this age. Her golden hairs ran down to just below her shoulders with few white tinges in between the hairs, thus providing a glimpse of her age. She was slim and attractive, her face was oval-shaped and she was slightly taller than her husband. However, her description will remain incomplete if I do not mention here anything about her eyes. Eyes, huh! They were blue like the sea but were completely still without any blinking and also the eyes had the appearance of those of a dead fish. Initially I was paying attention to our evening gathering and beautifully decorated rooms. The couple was very friendly to me and I grew fond of them within a short time. While Christopher walked me through his house, describing some special features, for a slight moment I had moved my head and met her eyes directly. I did not know why I looked towards her but what I noticed caused a chilling sensation run down my spine. I found her eyes were still with no emotions and expressions. She caught me noticing her eyes and immediately turned and looked away from me. I paid no further attention and tried to ignore the incident. I was wearing my favorite navy blue evening suit which I had purchased in London last year for special occasions. I found Christopher has already put up a party suit which looked expensive and his wife Martha (as far as I can recall her name) was dressed up in a pink and green evening gown. Martha also had put on some Indian style jewelry. She was very soft spoken. I came to know this day was very special to the couple as this was the day when they met each other.

The dinner served was excellent. After a long time I had ham, prawns and some fish. For dessert there was special strawberry custard pudding with some fruits and vanilla syrup. We drank the wine that I brought along with me. After quite some time I had such an elegant dinner. After dinner I accompanied Christopher to his study room while Martha stayed back for cleaning up dining table and dishes. The study room was smaller than other rooms. There were racks full of books which mainly encompassed literature, art and culture. This indicated Christopher was an avid reader and an aesthete. Christopher sat behind his desk while I dropped on a warm and comfortable sofa. Christopher lit his pipe. I was not at all interested in smoking and was eagerly waiting to hear his story. He started talking briefly about how he came to Bengal, how he met Martha, became close to each other and then how they got married. I was listening with care but was monotonous about those conversation topics and after a while lost interest. Christopher noticed this and asked me if something was wrong. The dinner was bit heavy for me. I did not attempt to start any new conversation and straightaway headed on to the main topic.

I straightly said, "I was wondering if you will like to illustrate about your experience regarding the Cursed Temple that you've mentioned last evening."

Christopher looked serious, "I personally did not have any experience, just heard about it and decided not to proceed further." He stopped for a while to dump some ash into his ashtray and then continued, "I'm surprised that you still have that in your mind."

I: "Well, as you can see, I cannot get this out from my mind. I need to know. This is something I've been looking for, I, I cannot explain properly. Something which is sort of thrilling and adventurous."

He: "This is not a good idea, at least from what I had heard."

I: "I had a motive behind my journey to India. I had been searching for something memorable, a kind of exploration which I can cultivate and take away with me."

He: "I warn you this is not at all something amusing. It can prove highly detrimental instead."

Life and destiny are quite strange and yet stranger are human beings. Having a premonition that something sinister is near to you, yet human being is automatically attracted towards it. That day if I had listened and followed Christopher's warning, I might rather have some different life.

He found me determined to know his tale. He dumped remaining ash into the ashtray, refilled with fresh tobacco in his pipe and started.

Christopher's Story

As you already know I was working in Indian railways. I had experience with railway tracks. I was into maintenance work. I had to collaborate with engineers and labors involved in this kind of work and see if there is any requirement and then same needed to be addressed on priority. This work required me to travel to different zones throughout India. One such instance came around six years ago, where I had to visit northern part of Bengal. I had to perform a lot of exhaustive work and needed to rest. On my way back to Calcutta, unfortunately I was infected by malaria and reluctantly had to spend few weeks for recovery, at Bolpur town in Birbhum. It was late in November that year when I was returning home and bitten by mosquito. Martha was not available in India at that time. She had to visit her maternal abode in Birmingham due health concerns of her mother. I stayed in touch with her through letters. During my period of illness some of the letters got skipped. After I recovered from malaria, I resumed writing letters to her but concealed my sickness and rather pretexted that I was quite busy in my work during those few weeks and did not get a chance to write her a letter. This was the only instance in my entire life that I had lied to her. Although my letters did not even reveal slightest hint about my illness, strangely enough she had guessed I was trying to hide something from her. May be it was her intuition or her affection towards me. Later on when she was back to India, I gave her the details and also apologized for hiding my illness from her. She was extremely sorrowful but that is a different story.

Let me focus on the main topic. Bolpur is a very nice town. It is located on the banks of Ajay and Kopai rivers. A nice place to spent few days for relaxation, it has fresh air and is extremely peaceful. In few days I became very fond of this place. When I arrived at Bolpur, my body was blazing with intolerant fever and I barely had any sense. I was rested in one of the railway quarter. I had a caretaker with me.

He brought a physician to my quarter. When the doctor visited my quarter, I was practically unconscious. After two days and two nights of high fever, fever slowly subsided. I was back to my feet but still weak enough to walk nicely. From time to time the local doctor will visit and monitor my health status. Luckily there was availability of Quinine, so treatment went well and I speedily progressed towards recovery. Even after completely recovering I decided to spent few more days at Bolpur and also take a trip of some nearby villages. The intention was to explore rural art and culture, as I already said I was fond of it.

Now, let me come up to the actual tale. I heard about some special art work at a quite village named Arghapur and decided to spend some time over there. Arghapur was situated nearly 50 miles from Bolpur and was not easily accessible. There was no rail route and no vehicle route. You need to either walk or depend on palanquin. In India palanquin is known as 'Palki', probably derived from some Sanskrit word. I had previous experience in travelling 'Palki'. I could have covered the 50 miles by walking. However, due to weak health after recovery and very less time in hand, as I had to return to Calcutta to report my work, I decided to hire 'Palki'. One cold morning in mid of December I set to sail. I had taken a bag with me which carried few clothes sufficient for 4-5 days and basket containing some food for lunch. In normal weather 50 miles would have taken approximately 20 hours to cover with breaks in between. But it was a bitter cold morning in December with dense fog and the palanquin bearers refused to leave early. Finally at mid-day when Sun was up and little of warmth prevailed, we left Bolpur. Initial five miles were covered very fast, then the road became very rough and the 'Palki' bearers started getting exhausted frequently. In the afternoon we stopped by a small village on the way to Arghapur and rested for 1 hour. I had my lunch and saved some for dinner. The 'Palki' bearers took break, had food and water and rested for a while. After 1 hour we left the village and headed towards Arghapur.

Slightly before sunset we reached a small wood. The 'Palki' bearers did not stop and went through it. The wood was not dense and looked quiet and peaceful. I lifted the curtain of 'Palki' and peeked outside. I nearly shouted and asked in their native language, Bengali, as why they did not rest and crossed the wood. I had learned Bengali and had a good hold of it during my long stay in Bengal. One of the 'Palki' bearers replied in Bengali "Babu, the forest is not safe. A Brahmadaitya lives here. After dark it attacks travellers." I laughed at his words. I said, "I do not believe. If truly there is Brahmadaitya, I would love to say Hello to him." At this point I should tell you what is a 'Brahmadaitya'. When an Indian Brahmin dies and turns into a demon, this is called 'Brahmadaitya'. I never believed in such things and laughed a lot. Few hours later, it was completely dark and the 'Palki' bearers stopped at a village. They informed that they'll not travel further at night due to fear of ghosts and dacoits. Even if ghosts and dacoits might spare them, snakes won't commit the same mistake. The 'Palki' bearers sounded quite funny. We found a nearby house and requested for shelter for that night. The owner was very kind and generous. He provided me a small room and 'Palki' bearers took place at the verandah. I consumed the food left from my lunch and drank water provided by the owner. The owner provided me a clean bed equipped with mosquito-curtain. This was more than sufficient to spend the cold and chilling night. I took my medicine and went to bed. Because of day long travel and also partly due to weakness from my recent illness I quickly fell asleep. Next day I woke up early from sweet chirping of some melodious bird. The Sun's rays flooded the room. I yawned and looked across the room. Although the room was small and revealed signs of poverty, still it was a splendid view in early morning. The owner of the house brought me some tea and snacks. I washed my face and cleaned my teeth and became busy with the meager breakfast. After an hour I was ready to leave. I thanked the owner and provided him my Calcutta address, suggested him whenever he needed any help from me, he can write to me or visit me at Calcutta. I'll be delighted to provide him help of any kind.

Shortly after, we left for Arghapur. The rest of the journey went well and we reached Arghapur in the afternoon just before the lunch time. I rented a small cottage which was easily accessible from the village's market. The rooms were decent although not spacious. The roof was made of straw, hay and bamboo. Overall it was quite comfortable and warm during winter. That evening I visited the village market and purchased few essential commodities to keep me going for 2-3 days. I did not intend to stay there for long, so purchased only the most basic items. Rest of the evening was uneventful.

In the morning I took a trip throughout the village surroundings, searching for some piece of art and craft that I can take back with me to Calcutta. I found few terra cotta works, wall hangings and few paintings from village market and few other places. In the afternoon, post lunch I took a walk by the side of the village's river bank, I would prefer to claim it as a stream rather than river. There was not much water in it. While strolling by the side of the river, at a distance I noticed a white structure which resembled a temple. It looked very nice from distance and I decided to take a closer look at it. This part was located outside the village and was deserted. The region where the temple was located was covered by some trees and shrubs which almost took the form of a small jungle. There was no sign of any life near about the temple. As I moved closer, the view of the temple became clearer. The temple was in a pretty bad shape. It had broken walls and branches of climbers and shrubs grew all over the broken walls almost concealing its true structure. I decided to go inside the temple to have a better look at it.

As I walked towards the temple and when was within few meters of it, suddenly I heard a warning note from behind. "Babu, please do not go there." I looked behind to find villager, old and thin. He said, "that place in cursed. Nobody goes there. That place was abandoned years ago."

I asked, "Why abandoned? What's in there?"

The man: "We do not speak about it. We avoid this place. Please go back from where you came from." I insisted him about telling me details but he kept on denying. He was hiding something from me. This raised my suspicions to a high level. He did not wait further and hurriedly went away. I will say he almost vanished within few seconds as if he was terribly frightened of something. I felt bit awkward about it. However, I decided not to step further towards the temple and returned to my cottage.

Later that evening, I asked about the temple to some villagers at the market. There was an old banyan tree at the center of the market place, where some villagers used to gather in the evening. It was place for their evening chat, leisure time, etc. I knew 1-2 of them. When I asked about the temple, they looked bit serious. From them I came to know that the temple was built around 100 years ago by some Zamindar. After building the temple, some very sinister events occurred. A curse fell on the Zamindar's family, some of his family members died suddenly of some unknown disease. The purohit (local priest) who was assigned to worship the holy shrine in that temple also suffered from quite misfortune. The temple was finally abandoned. I did not get any further details. It looked strange to me that like the local villager I met in the morning, they too hid something from me. I didn't understand what it was but it was certain that they were all scared of something. The people said that at night time still some evil things happened over there. Some claimed to have seen a young girl walking within the premises of the temple. People are afraid to go near to it, even in the day time. They seemed to believe that temple and its premises were inhabited by evil spirits. Few families in the village, who have lived in the village for more than hundred years, knew more details. Since, I did not have much time and my purpose was to collect some artwork, I was not interested and did not spend much time on story behind the temple. Although, I did not believe in them but still I had a strange terrorizing sensation in my heart.

Anyways, on the next day, I became busy collecting art items throughout the day and on the following day I left place. Before I left, for a while I felt like visiting the temple, the temple seemed to have some charm or like it had casted some spell on me. It was like as if the temple called me. This looked quite vague to me and I again had the same strange terrorizing sensation in my heart just like the day before. Anyhow I resisted the thought of visiting the temple and left the village. When I returned to Calcutta, Martha was already back to home from England. Sadly enough her mother had passed away. I informed her details about my malaria, my stay in Bolpur for a while but was careful about my visit to the village and kept this as a secret. When she learned about my illness she was pale and looked troubled. She felt sorry that she was away in the time of my need.

Chapter 5

Bolpur town! It's a strange human nature that human beings tend to overlook simple things of life which can bring enormous joy while giving value to false bigger aspects and then end up at nothing. I have been running after palaces, monuments, gardens and visited different cities of India of which I had heard lot of exquisite descriptions. I'm not saying that they were not worth visiting. However, the serenity of this small town carried me away. I felt that I was unknowingly running after luxurious boredoms while this small town brought a soothing feeling in heart for which I kept on hunting for days. Now I've reached this small town of which I was completely ignorant just two days before and this place brought me a different spice in my life. I do not undervalue the great Indian spots I visited, however this small town had something in it which gave ravishing refreshment to my heart.

After completion of Christopher's story that evening, I had asked him for some details and carefully jotted down each and every detail in my notebook that will help me through the journey. He was reluctant enough to provide me details and warned me several times. However, after listening to his tale I was more fascinated and was determined to know the secret behind the cursed temple. This was something for which I've been searching from a long time. With the help of his instructions and the notes I had taken that evening during our conversation, after two days I've successfully arrived at this town. I did not give up the small rented apartment back at Calcutta, as I was certain that I'll return after my expedition and will need it for few days for resting and future plans. I also had paid one month of advance to the landlord to block the apartment.

It was beginning of February 1937 and surprisingly the town had colder and a more chilling climate compared to Calcutta. With great difficulty I finally found and rented a local two bedroom flat near to railway station, good enough to spend few days. My next target was to find proper transportation to the village Arghapur. Why I was interested towards an adventure and how I had made up my mind to visit this place even after several warnings are redundant to discuss. When I expressed my interest to visit Arghapur , the landlord did not seem to bother much, however he looked a bit worried for unknown reason. As guided by Christopher, palki will be the best means to travel to the village. I inquired about same to the landlord and with his active contribution by that evening I was able to arrange for it. It was finalized that I would leave day after tomorrow, and that gave one full day in my hand to take brief trip around the Bolpur town. Next day, I visited the nearby river, took a walk by the river side and under the trees and rested for some time over there. Then I paid a visit to Shantiniketan, for which Bolpur is well known. The environment in Shantiniketan pleased me. Other places were not much worth mentioning, there was market place, small temples and residential areas as one would find in any small town. I returned to my room shortly after 8 PM, the roads were already nearly vacant and gave a ghostly feeling. Contrary to this situation, at this hour in Calcutta, streets will be well populated. The night was silent and even colder. Hoots of an owl residing in a nearby tree could be heard. Other than a few dogs barking on the street no sign of life can be sensed from outside the room. I had brought dinner from a local shop, which was not at all satisfactory. I longed for my native food. I went to bed early, since I had to rise early in the next morning.

Next morning, I rose up early and quickly got ready for the journey. I was happy that I had arranged all necessary aspects required for the journey in such a short span of time. I had purchased few dry food items from nearby shop on the previous day and also some I had brought from Calcutta. I intended to spend a few days at Arghapur, not sure for how long and so had made a quite an adequate arrangements for my stay there. The Palki and its bearers arrived before their scheduled time, quite appreciable. I did not reveal real purpose for my visit to Arghapur. I had just informed them that I was an art enthusiast and wanted to collect some local art items for my personal collection. The simple villagers easily believed in me. In fact, they looked overjoyed to know that I have come all the way from a foreign country to India with the intention to take a trip and collect rural cultural artworks. Within past few days I had mastered some more of the Bengali tongue and vocabulary. My sun-tanned skin quite dark by now, my brown eyes and my meager spoken Bengali almost concealed my true descent. This was beneficial for my stay, as on those days in India there were lot of rebels who might take me in a different way, although I meant no disregard and my sole purpose being expedition. Indians were struggling for freedom but that is not part of my story.

Anyways, the journey soon began. The Palki bearers travelled for about an hour and then took rest for few minutes. We passed by few villages on our way but did not halt anywhere for more than few minutes. Continuing this way, at around mid of the day we arrived at the small village which Christopher had mentioned in his tale. It looked we arrived a bit early from what Christopher had mentioned. The road to Arghapur had improved a bit as compared to what Christopher had mentioned in his tale, and so the Palki bearers were not much exhausted by the time they reached the village. The village's name was Chatna or Satna, I don't quite remember. It was very small and simple. Poverty was prevalent in the village. It only had few families left. Some huts looked almost empty and in a shape which one can observe after burning down. I was quite surprised at this view. I came to know from the Palki bearers that there was a cholera epidemic about two years ago which consumed many of the families. In those days Brahmins were honored a lot and had a separate status in the Indian society. The Brahmins from the village had given the idea that the village was possessed by some demon and the demon is hunting down families. So, they suggested burning down the huts and this would kill and prevent the demon from hunting further. Huts of the afflicted families were burned down mercilessly, and this also burned and killed many innocent people and sick people who could not escape the fire. A barbarian act indeed! The natives who managed to survive or ran away from the village, again re-built some huts. The Palki bearers halted near to a pond outside the village under a tree shade. I had my lunch and water inside the palki. I avoided the pond water, it might be contaminated. I then moved outside the palki, stretched my limbs and strolled around for a while. Shortly after, Palki bearer called me, "Babu please come back, we'll leave now. We need to cross Kataki's jungle before it is dark."

This was possibly the jungle Christopher had mentioned in his tale but didn't mention the name. I returned to the Palki and asked the bearer, "I have heard that there is a Brahmadaitya in that jungle. Can you tell me more about it?"

The bearer immediately closed his eyes and recited "Ram Ram, Ram Ram!" Then said "Babu we do not speak of it. Long time ago a Brahmin hanged himself and committed suicide there. From then on his ghost can be seen in the woods. His hanging body can be seen and no one travel's through it in the evening."

I said, "Suppose I demand to visit the jungle in the evening after sunset, will it be feasible for you? I'll pay you double the amount."

The Palki bearer strongly shook his head in disapproval, "No Babu, even if you pay us triple the amount we'll not take you through there after sunset. Please abandon the idea."

The strong determination in his eyes clearly informed me that none of them is going to support my idea to visit the jungle after dark. Reluctantly I had to abandon the lucrative sensation that I could have. Even while passing the jungle, the palki bearers increased their speed and hurriedly went passed it. For brief time while passing through the wood, I tried to have a good look of it as best as possible. It looked normal to me just like other woods I've heard or know. It had the similar vegetation as found in villages, only that they were denser in there. There were few trees, and I wondered which tree the Brahmin might have selected to commit suicide, just a curious idea. Had I encountered his spirit it would my first experience to greet a ghost.

Later that evening, when the Sun had disappeared and only faint moonlight prevailed, the Palki bearers called it a day and stopped at the village which Christopher had already mentioned suitable for night stay. This village was named Bongshigarh. In fact this village was quite bigger and more developed than the one I came across in the morning. There were even few well built houses apart from gorgeous huts. The houses were quite big and some looked luxurious as well, revealing signs of richness.

I had taken the address and details of the headman of the village from Christopher. I halted at his home. I introduced myself, told briefly about my purpose of travel, obviously a fake one, and informed him that I received his reference from Christopher. He was quite delighted. He shook hands with me. He made arrangements for my stay that evening and also made arrangements for the Palki bearers.

After dinner, the headman of Bongshigarh paid a visit to my room to ensure his guest was well attended. After he was satisfied, he enquired about Christopher, "I did not hear from Mr Christopher for a long time, it's been quite a few years now! Initially we used to exchange words via letters. Then suddenly 1 day letters stopped, not sure why. Is he okay, everything fine at his home?"

I said, "Yes everything is fine. He still remembers you." He looked pleased. He did not go into further conversation about Christopher and also seeing that I was pretty much tired from the journey, he retired from the room.

Next morning I left quite early. Before leaving, I thanked the headman a lot and tried to pay him for my stay. He politely rejected it. He said, "That I could be at your service is more than money or any material gift! I wish if you could have stayed for some more time, so that I could have provided you a better service."

I replied, "This is remarkable! I can dream of nothing more. I'll always remember you, even when I return to my homeland." He looked pleased.

The remaining of journey went well and I reached Arghapur before afternoon. At first glance Arghapur appeared more like a town rather than a village. Probably it had developed rapidly compared to the time when Christopher had visited. The market area was congested and it looked like a congregational place for villagers from nearby villages. There was trading of rice, vegetables, fish, chicken, eggs, clothes and many more. The market place had a warm climate, compared to rest of the village and people looked extremely busy. This clearly revealed that Sunday was trading day in Arghapur market.

It took a while for me to arrange for a room to stay for a few days. People did not seem quite interested in knowing my purpose of visit. I rented a flat in a three-storeyed house, away from the market place. It took around 25-30 minutes of walk from the market to the house. The house was very recently built, around 2 years ago and so was clean and decent looking. This part of Arghapur was almost vacant and only few houses could be seen, mostly newly built place. Coconut, neem and mango trees in this part of the town could also be seen. Weather was cool and refreshing. Unfortunately, there was no nearby shop and I had to walk down to the market place to purchase any item I needed.

My flat was in the first floor. It consisted of two bed rooms, a partial arrangement for kitchen or rather a kitchenette and one bathroom. The rooms were almost empty of any furnishing except for 1 bed and a table and chair set. I would have to find a cook who can prepare meals for me. Raw vegetables fish, meat and eggs can be easily purchased from the market. I felt it would be a hard time to spend a few days here as it was like rebuilding a new place of accommodation. I didn't engross myself into the rebuilding thoughts of the place, quickly unpacked my bags and orderly placed the temporary amenities. I had already requested for some hot water for bathing to the caretaker of the house. In the entire house, I was the only resident apart from the caretaker and his family. The caretaker and his family resided at one corner in the ground floor and occupied few rooms. He had a son and three daughters. The daughters and son were married. The son owned a small shop at one end of the market and lived with the caretaker. The caretaker was short-heighted and above 60 years old. He was born and brought up here and so knew Arghapur from his child hood days. I was pleased, as this would be golden opportunity for me to know details from him about the Cursed temple.

While I was unpacking my luggage, the caretaker knocked on the door. He called me, "Babu, hot water is ready. I brought it in a bucket." I opened the door and took hold of the bucket and then transferred it to the bathroom. There were only two buckets and one mug in the bathroom. The caretaker was waiting by the door. I asked him, "I'll require some arrangement for food at least twice a day."

He immediately replied by putting up a gesture that indicated assurance, "This can be arranged. My wife and daughter in law can cook food for you and I can bring this up to your room. You absolutely need not worry about anything. We'll get vegetables, eggs, meat, chicken or whatever food items you like and take care of the cooking part. We also have a spare cutlery set, plates and bowl. All this will cost you very less. We do not have any visitors at this part of Arghapur, your stay here will be peaceful."

I've already mentioned to the caretaker about my purpose of stay as an art collector and an author. The landlord stayed in a house close to the market and was a rich man, as per the villagers. For me he looked very simple to at first glance, without any complexity and was a man of few words. When he heard that I had visited for art collection and authoring an article on the village art, he easily believed in me and looked overjoyed. He charged me very meager amount for few days. He told, "For now this is sufficient. If you wish to stay longer, we can settle the outstanding sum later on. All the rooms in the house are vacant except for the ground floor, where you'll find the caretaker. I had built the house for my son, who stays in Delhi for his job. He rarely visits Arghapur." Saying this he handed me over the keys with trust. The landlord's servant guided me to the house and explained the old caretaker about purpose of my visit and informed that I'll stay here for few days. The caretaker's name was Hari Das. His son's name was Mahadeb.

Hari stood at the door looking at me intently while I was preparing myself for the bath. I looked at him and understood that he wished for some advance. He was old, most of his hairs had grown white and wrinkles were all over his face and across his forehead. However, he physically looked strong and healthy. I took out my wallet and handed over some money to him. I asked him, "If this is not sufficient, then let me know."

He immediately put his tongue out and touched his ears with both hands, as if he had done a terrible mistake, "This is very high amount. You need not worry for meals for at least a week. Also, if you want something else, please let me know. We are always at your service."

I had a thought pestering my mind, why not ask him about the Cursed Temple. While Hari made a move to go away, I exclaimed, "Hey Hari! Is there any river in this place."

Hari's face brightened up, "Yes yes Babu! There is a small river flowing at the north east part of this village. At this time of the year it is almost dry. It gets filled up during rainy season. The river's name is Mohna!"

I asked, "Is there any temple near to this river? I mean, I've heard about a temple which is cursed."

Immediately brightness in his expression vanished and he turned white. He said in a dry voice, "We do not speak of it. It is not a good place. There is a tale behind it. Please rest now Babu. I can tell you the shortest route to the river, you can visit there in the evening but I'll advise you not to go near to the temple. Also, please return home before it is dark." After saying these words in a single breath, he did not wait further comments and hurriedly went away. My doubts remained unanswered. I wondered what's so scaring about this temple, why it is cursed and why these people do not speak about it. The more I thought about it, more I went into dilemma and even more determined to know the secret behind this temple. I have to know about the past behind this temple and why local residents avoided it. Anyways, I planned to take a stroll down the river this evening and during that time take a trip of this temple.

Chapter 6

I had my lunch and went to rest. I didn't realize when I fell asleep. When I woke up, the Sun was already setting down. I quickly got up from the bed and moved to the washroom to freshen up. Within no time I was ready to visit river Mohna. I took a small handbag with me which contained a powerful torch, a few small medical equipment like scalpel to collect any interesting sample and a small box to store the sample.

Before leaving the house I informed Hari that I'll be going to the market and a little bit late for dinner. He believed me and made no comments. After about half an hour of travel and enquiring a few local pedestrians I reached the west side of the river Mohna. On the other side of the river, a dense jungle appeared and I could not see through it. Melodious chirping of different unknown birds filled the atmosphere with a pleasant feeling. I'm not good at recognizing birds so could not make out to which species the birds belonged.

The river looked shallow as Hari had predicted that it would be, at this time of year. As I moved upstream by the side of the river, from some distance a small wood could be seen in front of me. This small wood looked distinct from the dense one present on the other side. However, possibly this small wood could be an extension of the dense one. I had no idea. Anyways, I started walking towards the small wood in front of me, which supposedly shaded the temple as Christopher had told me.

Shortly after, I was able to see the temple. It was a white structure and built with great efforts from what it appeared. Due to lack of maintenance it had become dilapidated and most of its parts were covered with climbers and shrubs. The top portion of the temple was narrower than the rest of the portion and still in good shape. The top portion of the temple steeply rose to take the form of a narrow tower, a typical amongst the temples found in northern India. This is called shikhara. I've visited temples which were built with several shikharas, while this temple had only one. It was a small structure nothing interesting. The small wood had few mango trees, palm trees, and I could also make out people and neem trees. Bushes and shrubs grew all around the temple giving it an untidy look. It seemed different species of uncommon plants grew in this area, which I did not find in any other villages I had already visited. I did not know the names of these but they were certainly not something commonly seen. Possibly someone might have planted them particularly in this area.

I could not see the entrance to the temple, probably it was on the other side and I was behind the temple. The garbhagriha or the sanctum which housed the shrine will then be supposedly visible from the other side. This actually made sense. If the temple was built as south-facing, then I was standing towards north of the temple and so I could see only the temple from behind. Till now I didn't know to which holy shrine this temple was dedicated. Whoever I had asked about this temple, all of them have refused to discuss any further. The major detail which I had known till now was provided to me by Christopher. Now, the live structure was in front of me. I did not find anything awkward about the temple. It looked quite calm and abandoned from distance. There was no sign of any life near about the temple.

As I walked towards the temple, it grew larger in view. Within about 15 yards of the temple I realized it was actually a quite bigger than my expectation. It was possibly 25 feet or more high and about 30 feet or more in breadth. It had few stair cases at the bottom. Shortly after then, I entered the wood and in front of me stood the enormous temple. I quickly climbed the steps and came up to a platform built of stone. The temple actually stood at one end and this was the start of the platform. Rest of the platform was empty. It did not make any sense to me why such a platform was built and why the temple was placed at one end. Possibly there were plans to build other similar temples or some other structures on the same platform, who knows. I moved towards the front side of the temple and was able to locate the entrance as I had anticipated. The entrance had a solid doorway, although one panel had broken down. The other panel was closed or open, I could not make out at first. It was almost dark now, the last rays of the Sun fell on the temple. Due to presence of wood and shrubs within temple premises, light was scarce compared to the river bank and I could not see very clearly. I took out my torch and looked around at the premises. There were bushes all around and few mango, neem and banyan trees. The inside of the temple was dark and I could not see inside.

I waved the torch light to other areas to have a good look of the surroundings. Behind the shrubs, bushes and trees some ruins appeared at a distance. I could not clearly make out what the ruins were. From distance it looked like as if it was a palace or some similar structure sometime. The structure was located exactly opposite to the temple door. Due to dense plants, the ruins got hidden from my view previously and also it was not visible from below the platform or from the river bank. The ruins were bit far away and my intention to visit this place was due to the temple, so I ignored the ruins and focused on the temple.

I flashed the torch light at the temple entrance to have a good view of inside. Surprisingly, the entrance was quite neat and clean, as if someone uses the entrance and cleans it. There was little sign of dirt. The door was solidly built and the panel which was still intact, was wide open, as if someone has opened it up recently. I steadily stepped inside the temple. Inside the temple I could see solid brick walls covered with little bit of shrubs and some spider webs. The density of shrubs was comparatively lesser inside than outside, as if someone cleans up the inner portion of the temple regularly. Already when I was within a stone's throw distance to the temple, I could sense a strange odour. Now, the odour became stronger and I realized it was very pungent. I had smelt similar odours in other temples I had visited but this was more pungent and somewhat different. I could not make out what exactly it was. It gave me a sick and intoxicating sensation.

Slowly I crossed the doorway and stepped inside. The smell became yet stronger. The garbhagriha, which is the sanctum that houses the holy shrine in the temples, was located towards the right. There was a small entrance to it. The inside of the temple was cold and humid. It was surprisingly clean. I rotated the torch light to my left and right to have a better look of the temple from inside. The entire temple was empty except for the garbhagriha. After a while I realised a faint beam of light radiated from inside the garbhagriha, not sure why I was not able to see that previously.

Slowly I moved towards the garbhagriha to see the holy shrine. The smell grew even stronger and stronger. By now I had started feeling dizzy. I stood outside the garbhagriha and shoved the torch light inside it. The faint beam of light came from an oil lamp from inside the garbhagriha. From the faint beam of light the holy shrine appeared to be of goddess Kali. I highlighted my torch light on the holy shrine to have a better look. Indeed it was goddess Kali. The shrine was neat and clean, and looked new and was nicely carved out of stone. There were some flowers and china roses placed below it and the shrine was wearing a garland made of china roses. Astonishingly, all the flowers and garland looked fresh. I wondered if this was abandoned place, then who came here to worship. I did not see any sign of human life within the temple premises. From where did these flowers come? I was confused. As I observed the holy shrine carefully and in more details, I became horrified. On the tongue of the shrine there was a fresh red tinge which resembled blood. Not only was that, below the shrine there also were fresh drops of blood. I was not sure from where the blood came. Also, eyes of the shrine were quite lively. I felt like the shrine was watching me. My heart started beating rapidly. I had a chilling and shocking sensation running down my spine.

Not sure what to do, I moved one step forward towards the holy shrine. I was determined to check if it was truly blood or something else. Suddenly a soft and sweet voice close behind startled me. It was a female voice. The sound was very close. I tried to immediately flash the torch light behind me to see who was there. More to my amazement, no one was there! I focused the torch light everywhere possible and searched all over the place again and again but did not find anyone. There was pin-drop silence around the temple. I again highlighted the torch light over the shrine and was even more horrified. I could not find the drops of blood! Blood has vanished! I rubbed my eyes with one hand but no use. There was no blood. The shrine also seemed to have lost its liveliness and looked quite old and worn out. More surprisingly the flower have vanished too! I started sweating profusely. Terrified and confused, I tried to figure out what was happening.

The pungent smell was all over the air and caused me immense dizziness. I felt as if I was going to faint. I could no longer stand on my feet. I needed fresh air. With great difficulty I tried to rush outside. Once I was out in the fresh air, I was gasping for breath. After a while, when I was bit stable, I tried to recollect what exactly happened inside. Suddenly, I had a strange feeling that someone was watching me. I waved my torch beam in front of me. Within a blink of an eye something moved away. I could not understand what it was. It was a gigantic figure and hairy. Not sure if it was human or any kind of animal. I kept on rotating the torch light but could see no one.

I declared in my mind that this was sufficient for one day. I could take no more. It was already dark and moon light was faint. I was quite drowsy by now, barely able to stand on my feet. Gathering full strength, I ran outside the temple premises and kept on running by the side of the river, until I was quite far away from the temple. Suddenly, I stepped on a stone or something similar and fell down. I hurt right side of my head. I tried to feel the injury with one hand but did not feel any strength. I saw someone approaching towards me. This was the last thing I could remember. Gradually darkness filled my eyes and I started to lose my senses. Shortly after, I lost consciousness.

Chapter 7

I woke up sensing strong rays of Sunlight flooding my room. I gradually rose up and sat on my bed. I slowly gathered my senses and tried to recall my experience. There was a jar of water and a glass on the table beside the bed. I poured a glass of water and drank all of it in a single gulp. This brought me some relief and refreshed my mind. I had brought a small clock along with me from England, which used to be my father's. I had kept it at one corner of the only table in the room, beside my bed. On the first day I had moved that table near to my bed and by the side of window. I preferred it that way. I could sit by the table and look through the window as long as I wished. This helped me to think, plan and come up with innovative thoughts and ideas, although full of risks. I looked at the clock to find it was already 1 PM.

I touched right part of my head which I expected to be injured. To my surprise, there was no injury. I touched and rubbed different parts of my skull but did not find any sign of injury. There was also no pain! How long I had been unconscious? How did I come to my room? As I was wondering on all these thoughts, a young man in early thirties came to my room. He looked familiar. Initially I could not make out who he was or where I've seen him previously. After a while, I realised he must be Mahadeb, son of Hari. His figure resembled to his father's to a great extent but he was bit taller, I guess. That explained why he looked familiar to me initially.

I made first statement, "You must be Mahadeb, son of Hari."

He said, "That's right babu. How are you feeling now?"

I felt much better, the dizziness had completely vanished, except that I still felt a little bit of tiredness. "I'm better now. How did I come here? What happened? How long I've been unconscious?"

Mahadeb replied, "Yesterday evening a villager found you outside the Cursed Temple, lying below the staircases leading to the temple premises. You've remained unconscious for entire night and day. It's afternoon now."

I felt stupefied. I asked, "Below the staircases?" I paused a little and said, "If I clearly remember, I had visited the temple last evening. I ran out of the temple and moved far away from it. While running I stepped on a stone or something and fell down."

He strangely looked at me, "The villager found you lying on the grass, below the staircases. You were in deep sleep. He had seen you previously in this house. With the help of few of his fellows, he brought you here."

If I clearly remember, I had run far away from the temple and by the side of the river. I could not think of how I reached to the temple staircases. Everything looked mysterious.

Mahadeb said, "Father had warned you. You did not listen to him. Consequences could have been severe. With God's grace you are safe."

I: "I want to know more about the temple. I'll pay for that".

Mahadeb: "It's not about the payment. We do not speak of the temple. It is cursed."

I: "Anyways, I will like hear the details behind it. I'm curious about it. It does not allow me to sleep. It haunts me in my dreams. I need to know. Please understand I'm a traveller and an author. My journey will remain incomplete if I do not know about the temple".

Mahadeb: "I myself do not know much about the temple. My father knows more details. He was born and brought up here and has lived here his entire life. My ancestors also lived here. I'll inform him regarding your wish. For now please take bath and have some food. After that you must take rest. You are most fortunate that you are still alive. Till now, whoever have tried to visit the temple have either died of mysterious death or have become paralyzed."

This caused me some anxiety. I asked, "Why is this so? What is the curse on this temple?"

Mahadeb: "From what I have heard, long time ago, a Pir visited that place. He was treated very badly. He cursed on that place. Bad omen followed then on".

I: "When did this happen, any idea?"

Mahadeb: "More than 100 years ago, from what I had heard. My father will know better. For now, please don't think about it. My father would tell you in the evening".

He stopped there and did not go into further conversation. He looked worried about me. I pulled a clean towel from my bag and went into the washroom. There was a bucket of water and a mug. I felt the water with my right index finger and it felt warm. Probably Mahadeb or Hari had brought it some time ago. As it was beginning of February, the climate was still cold, it had readily cooled down the water in the bucket. Nevertheless, the water was still good enough for me and I mostly preferred lukewarm water for bathing. This bath will rejuvenate me and I'll be back to normal. The events from last evening were causing great anxiety to me. I could not think of any logical way of how I reached back the temple staircases. I clearly remember to have ran away from the temple. All of it looked so enigmatic and the more I thought about it, more I became confused. There is no possibility that physically I could have reached back the staircases of the temple unless someone dragged me there. Also, I remembered to hurt the right portion of my skull. Surprisingly, there is no sign of any injury or even pain.

After bath, I quickly changed my clothes. I can sense terrible hunger build up in my stomach. This indicated it was no time to think about semantics and indulge myself into grave confusing thoughts. One thing was clear. I was unharmed. This gave me some inspiration.

I found meal was already waiting on the table. Meal comprised of rice, chapattis, vegetables, dal and chicken curry. I also found few pieces of freshly cut onion. The rice was hot and steaming, so was the dal and curry. I abandoned further thoughts and voraciously attacked the food.

Within no time it was all empty. I burped loudly. This was a bad habit which I had developed in India among others. I washed my hands and cleaned my mouth in the same bowl where Hari had put curry. Another bad habit indeed! Contented from the heavy meal, I went to sleep and within no time possibly started snoring.

Chapter 8

I woke up to find Sun had already set and it was completely dark outside except for faint light coming from the moon. The Moon appeared as a slender crescent on the sky. Probably New Moon phase was near. My room was lightened by the light from a hurricane lamp placed on one side of my table. The light from the lamp was powerful enough to illuminate my entire room and the faint moon light which fell inside the room through the window was almost invisible. The window was closed and the moon light entered the room via the window glass. I rose up on my bed, yawned a little. For a while I wondered what to do and then lifted up myself from the bed, went to the washroom and freshened up. I was feeling fresh and energetic.

After a while Hari entered my room with tea and some snacks and gently put them down on the table. He looked pale. He spoke in a weak voice, "Babu, you should not have visited that temple. You are lucky that you are still alive."

I replied, "I could not hold myself. Your warnings and made me more enthusiastic about the temple. I want to know more details about this temple. It will be an interesting tale to add in my book."

Hari stared at my eyes for a while as if searching for something and after a while said calmly, "Well then, let me tell you the story behind this temple. Please listen patiently". I sat down on my bed while Hari found a place for himself on the floor near to the table.

Hari's Tale – The establishment of Arghapur

The major part of the story I had heard was from my grandfather and rest from here and there. Long time ago, this place used to be a small village surrounded by a dense wood, most of which you'll still be able to see on the eastern side of river Mohna. Please excuse me as I cannot recall what was the name of the village at that time. The village was inhabited by poor farmers and their families who made their living mainly on paddy they used to grow outside the village lands. The dense wood used to be the den for a band of fierce and merciless dacoits. Nevertheless the dacoit troop never disturbed the village as they clearly knew farmers were very poor and nothing could be obtained from them.

The dacoits used to attack any traveller that passed by the woods and seize their belongings and treasury. If the traveller tried to refuse or revolt, the dacoits simply split their throat. This land was notorious for this band of dacoits. As slowly time passed by, travellers came to know more about this place and they scarcely used this region to travel. However, every now and then someone might make mistake to take this route and became the unfortunate victim of the dacoits. Since, the travellers were becoming scarce day by, it became difficult for the dacoits to survive. One day a traveller unknowingly used this route. This traveller happened to be a cousin, a distant brother of Raja Arghapratap Roy from north of Bengal. He had purchased some jewelry and precious garments from a distant land and was going to gift this to Raja Arghapratap.

While travelling towards north of Bengal, the traveller lost his way and unfortunately took this jungle route. He had very few guards and travelled in a palki. It was almost evening time and Sun was setting down when they were inside the wood. While they were travelling by the side of the river, the band of dacoits suddenly stormed into them. The dacoits quite outnumbered the guards and so they could not stand the attack of the dacoits. Within no time the guards fell and were defeated. The dacoits slaughtered almost all the guards except one who luckily escaped. The traveller, Raja Arghapratap Roy's cousin showed resistance and was mercilessly killed in the battle. The guard who escaped was badly wounded and took shelter within the village. The dacoits searched for the wounded guard for days but could not find him. The villagers hid him well and denied his presence. Thinking that the guard must have died dacoits stopped further searching.

After the wounded guard healed up, he expressed gratitude to the villagers and departed. He directly travelled to Raja Arghapratap Roy's palace from there. Once he reached the palace, without any delay he straightaway went to Raja and detailed him about the dacoit invasion, about the battle and how his cousin bravely fought but was mercilessly killed. Initially, Raja was quite, shocked and mourned for a while. After he came out of his mourning, he decided to punish the bandits and that these dacoits need to be eliminated for travellers' safety. Raja Arghapratap had an enormous panel of soldiers, who were expert swordsmen, Lethels (Indian "bo" staff fighters) and archers. The guard gave an estimate of the number of dacoits. Raja Arghapratap Roy immediately made a decision to quash the dacoits and put them to death.

Raja Arghapratap took the details of the dacoits from the guard, figured out a rough idea about the number and skillsets of the dacoits. Accordingly, he assembled some of the best men in his troop, each soldier were disguised so that no one recognized them as a soldier. They left for the jungle that night. They had sufficient supplies to survive for over two weeks. They did not take horses and travelled on foot, so that it would not alert the dacoits. Before they left, they offered prayer to Goddess Kali to crush the dacoits. Raja Arghapratap was himself a devotee of Goddess Kali. The army travelled rapidly by road, rested only for few hours each day. Raja himself assumed the disguise of a native villager. Under his breath he was vindictive and calmly preparing to mutilate the band of dacoits and put them to death.

After three days of tiresome travel, they reached the village and near to the jungle. They took shelter in the village and rested for the day. The Raja had an excellent spy within his panel of soldiers, who can easily climb up trees, hold breath under water for long time and was trained to perform numerous other activities which otherwise is not possible for a normal human being. The spy was also obedient to the Raja. He ordered his spy to secretly keep a watch on the dacoits over the next two days and inform him about their every minute detail. Based on his master's instructions, the spy travelled secretly towards the jungle. He hid on the tree tops, moved from tree to tree and finally reached near to the dacoits' den. Over the next two days, he took shelter on a tree top and observed every activity of the dacoits in minute details. When he was satisfied, he silently moved back to the village to report back to the Raja.

As soon as Raja got the information on the dacoits, he decided to attack them that very night at mid night. That night the soldiers, disguised, armed with deadly weapons, silently moved towards the jungle. Upon reaching the jungle the army split into three parts. The plan was that two groups would quietly surround the dacoits while the third group would attack them from behind. The Raja took the lead of the third attacking group. As per plan, two groups surrounded the dacoits quietly and stationed at appropriate places. Post that they signaled the attacking group. The attacking group then moved rapidly and posed an unannounced strike on the dacoits. The dacoits were mostly sober at that time, unarmed and were shocked by this sudden unanticipated strike. They barely stood a chance against the skilled army. Majority of the dacoits were killed, those that tried escape were caught by the two surrounding group of soldiers and were put to death. The few remaining surrendered themselves.

The Raja departed from the jungle with the captives and victory. It was beginning of a new morning. The once dreaded troop of bandits had no more existence. Sun just started rising in the sky as if declaring and rejoicing Raja's victory. The Raja and his troop rested by the river Mohna in the morning. He decided to take a walk around the place. The jungle was thin and was merely a wood on other side of the river. The Raja swam across the river to the other side to take a good look at the place. The serenity of the place and delectable land filled the Raja's heart with great pleasure and joy. Within minutes he took the decision to build a palace over here and develop and transform the small village into a township. The Raja and his troop left the village on same day but his heart and soul remained here. Before leaving the village, he expressed gratitude to the villagers for providing shelter and the great help they had done. He also revealed his ideas to the local people. The simple villagers were overjoyed to know about Raja's future plans; they supported him and blessed him for demolishing the band of ferocious dacoits. These happened a long time ago, may be 200 years or more. To honour Raja and his work this land was named after him as Arghapur. This was how Arghapur town came into existence. It slowly then transformed from a mere village into a flourishing business township.

Chapter 9

After telling the story behind how Arghapur was set up and Raja's tale of destroying the dacoits without break, Hari stopped for a while. He yawned, he looked bit tired may be because of his old age. He was sitting on the ground on an Indian mattress folding his legs towards his chest and resting his hands on the knees. After he spoke about Arghapur's establishment he released his legs and assumed a relaxed posture. He then looked outside the closed window, inspecting the darkness and the faint beam that radiated from the Moon. Probably the actual tale was to begin and he had a pretty worried expression over his visage. He was possibly deciding on how to move further in his tale. I had changed my position from the bed and was now sitting on the chair by the table and smoking a cigar after many days. He then progressed with further part of the story.

Hari's Tale – Story behind Cursed Temple

About 80 years ago, before I was born, this temple was built. At that time Raja Samarjit Roy was the ruler of Arghapur. He was the great grandson of Raja Arghapratap Roy. Raja Samarjit Roy did not have any children. His first wife died of tuberculosis. His second wife did not bear him any child and showed no signs of conception. The doctors almost gave up. Raja Samarjit was growing old and was becoming worried. He was a very decent man. Unlike his great grandfather, he was not a warrior and more inclined to art, craft and music.

Raja Arghapratap had built a palace by the side of the river Mohna. You can still see few remains of this palace little bit away from the temple, at a walking distance from the temple. Raja's four generations have dominated over this town. Raja had almost closed his connection with northern part of Bengal where he had the other palace. He had transferred the region of the northern part of Bengal, Zamindari, his palace and his almost entire panel of workers to his younger brother and came down to Arghapur to establish a new rule. He had retained a few trustworthy workers and soldiers with him. He built this palace at Arghapur around 200 years ago. He hired new workers, servants and soldiers for his new palace.

Coming back to Raja Samarjit Roy, he had tried almost all possibilities so that his wife can bear him a child. Day after day passed by, Raja Samrajit Roy was growing old but there seemed to be no hope. One day a sage person suggested him to visit Varanasi and give offerings to Lord Vishwanath. The wish for a child will become true. Raja Samarjit obeyed this suggestion and accordingly paid a visit to Varanasi and Lord Vishwanath. His dream was finally fulfilled. One day Rani conceived and they were blessed with a baby boy.

Celebrations and donations proceeded following this and Arghapur saw biggest events of all times. Lot of entertainers from distant lands visited and from morning to evening there was an atmosphere of enjoyment and celebrations. Shops were closed, businesses came to a standstill. Days passed by in happiness. The Raja became holy and paid occasional visits to Indian temples. Few years later the Rani again conceived. Brahmins felt this is a God's gift and the Raja should thank God in a different manner. This will bring a fortune to the land and the empire. They suggested Raja Samarjit to build a temple dedicated to Goddess Kali.

Raja Samarjit accepted the suggestion and started working towards it. He selected a small region on the eastern side of the river bank to develop the temple. This place was near to the Raja's palace. From the temple platform one could still see the palace ruins. He hired skilled labourers and sculptors to build this temple, who came from northern part of Bengal. The holy shrine of Goddess Kali was brought from eastern part of Bengal. The shrine was built by a very skilled and renowned sculptor. The temple construction started on the planned date. It went well. Within a year major part of the temple was built. Gradually the temple tower stood and the garbhagriha was constructed inside this. The temple construction slowly reached towards completion without any hurdle.

Then one day a Pir visited the town. Unknowingly he reached the eastern part of the river Mohna. After travelling for a while he reached the temple site. It was almost evening and the Sun had settled down with last rays illuminating the temple premises. The temple site was empty that time and the labourers had departed for the day. He was tired, thirsty and hungry. He felt to take rest for the day within the temple premises. He drank river water and went inside the temple in the hope of finding a shelter. The temple shikhara was newly built and still some part of it was under construction. The temple was deserted, the labours had retired for the day, so he thought no one as around to disturb. Climate was hot and he was exhausted. He felt it as an ideal spot to spend the night and resting inside the temple will also protect him from wild animals if any were there in the woods. Also, the temple premises were soothing and he felt relaxed inside the temple. He carried his belongings in a small bag. He used the bag as a pillow and went to sleep.

Early next day morning he woke up abruptly. He felt great pain in his belly and opened his eyes. He found a man savagely kicking him in the belly. Immediately he came to his senses and moved away from this brutal act. Other parts of his body had bruises to and he hold down his belly to control the pain. He stared at the man. Feebly he asked the reason for this inhuman act.

The man replied, "I'm the temple supervisor and the Raja will not entertain any beggars to use this place".

Pir said, "You could have alerted me in a gentle way. There is no reason for this kind barbarian act. I want to speak to your king".

The supervisor laughed and mocked at him, "Who do you think you are, Old beggar! And why would the king like to meet a vagabond. This is not a public property that anyone can come inside and use it. This temple and the entire land belong to Raja. He can do whatever he feels like. He'll surely not encourage any unwanted intruders in his temple pemises".

Pir said, "O monster, have pity on the poor. The temple is a holy place and God is for all. I'm sure your king will not like such wicked act".

The argument went for a while. That day's work came to standstill. The Raja was soon informed about the incidence. He became angry.

He immediately approached the temple. By that time, the Pir had moved outside the shikhara. He was further tortured by the temple supervisor and other men working there. Upon reaching the temple, Raja found Pir near to the newly built staircases. He summoned his men and asked further details. He was furious with rage.

Raja asked the Pir, "What nonsense is this? Why did you come here? This is a holy place, abode for shrine of Goddess of Kali. I'm not building this temple for vagabonds like you to rest".

Pir said, "O great, kind king, have mercy on poor. Temple is God's place and God is for all. Yesterday evening I was tired and found this place. I had no other place to go. Also, it was dark and the woods have wild animals. So, I took shelter inside the temple for just the evening. Please be considerate."

Raja was more furious, "You filthy, old beggar! Leave this place immediately or I'll have my men thrashed you away".

The Pir pleaded for mercy but the Raja showed none. Wounded, tired, tortured and humiliated, he left the place. But before he left, he terribly cursed the Raja, the workers and the temple. He said, "You barbarians, God will never forgive you! All of you will suffer. May the curse of Goddess Kali fall upon you and your children! You will never be able to worship in this temple. The temple's holy shrine will never accept your prayer. Whoever will try to worship in this temple will be subjected to the curse and will be destroyed".

Raja's men laughed at this and did not pay attention to the Pir. They resumed their normal day's work. The Raja too ignored the Pir's words and felt those were the words of a beggar, what harm can they do! He did not take any action against the Pir, since this happened at the temple premises, a holy place, and ordered his men to resume with their work. As the days passed by, the temple's work progressed steadily and nothing happened. The workers and the Raja almost forgot the incident. Then one day, during midday, a block of stone from top of the temple fell upon a worker. The worker died immediately. The other workers were terrified. It happened all of a sudden and no one knew, what was the exact cause that the block of stone fell from such a great height. When the stone block fell, no one was working at the temple top, the work at that portion had already completed. There was no chance that any block of stone was incorrectly positioned at that place or could have been misplaced. All the workers were horrified and recalled the Pir's curse, they presumed the curse had begun. The Raja visited the spot and after learning about the incident, simply ignored it. He felt it was just an accident and that some lazy worker might have positioned the stone block incorrectly, which might had been misplaced due to encountering strong winds day by day. He declared this was just an accident and had nothing to do with Pir's curse. The workers were still frightened and reluctant to resume with their work. Seeing resistance from the workers, Raja decided to increase their wages and immediately announced the same. Also, he asked his accountant to provide some compensation to the worker's family who died of the accident. The poor workers could not give up the lucrative offer and resumed their work. However, they remained scared internally.

Situations looked normal thereafter, and day by day the temple work then progressed rapidly and lot of the parts were built including the platform, staircases, only some little work inside the temple, shikhara and garbhagriha still remained. No misfortune occurred indicative of the curse, except small incidents like slipping and falling down with no major injuries, misplacement of equipment, etc. Everybody felt those were normal during building work and ignored the same. The Raja decided to establish the shrine and start worshipping before the temple was completely built. The workers took a break from their work for a few days, by then earned a lot and went away to their residents to meet their family. All seem to have practically forgotten the mysterious death incident and took it for granted that it was due to an accident. Only the temple supervisor stayed back. The supervisor decided to stay beside the temple for few days, so as to guard the temple until a suitable purohit or family priest was selected to worship the temple shrine. One of Raja's men from his army squad also stayed back along with supervisor. It was decided that the supervisor would take shelter in a temporary tent built beside the temple, while the guard will remain assembled outside the temple door to ensure that no one breaks into the temple. The temple door was opened once in the morning for some time to clean up and kept locked for rest of the day.

First two nights went passed normally. On the third night, at around midnight the guard heard a strange noise from inside the temple. He quickly rose up from his bed and found the temple door was locked. He felt, he might be dreaming, did not bother further and went back to sleep. Next night, again at around midnight he heard this strange noise from inside the temple and this time it was more prominent. He felt as if someone from inside the temple was belly-laughing like trying to mock someone. It was a female voice. The temple door was locked as usual and so there was no chance that anyone could have trespassed and gone inside. The guard was scared and nervous. He quickly walked towards the tent and woke up the supervisor. He informed him about this incidence. The supervisor refused to believe the guard and thought he might be dreaming. However, the guard was persistent. The supervisor used to keep the temple door key below his pillow. Seeing that the guard is stubborn, he reluctantly picked up the key and went towards the temple door. The guard followed him with a lamp.

The door lock was made of bronze and it was heavy. It took some effort to unlock for an unknown reason, as if something was resisting it to open, although the lock was new and properly greased. The supervisor felt bit strange but did not express any concern. They went inside the temple and waved the lamp light in all possible directions to see if anyone or anything was there but no one was found. They searched all possible places but found no one. There was not even a slightest chance that someone could have escaped their vision and hid somewhere inside the temple. In fact there was no such place to hide inside the temple. They then moved towards the garbhagriha to check if the holy shrine was properly covered or not. The holy shrine was intended to be uncovered following certain rituals and only on the day of first worship. They found the holy shrine was covered but looked bit untidy as if someone has disturbed the cover. The supervisor and guard looked at each other but could not make out of what possibly could have led to this. The guard then focused the lamp light all over inside the garbhagriha. Suddenly he screamed and alerted the supervisor. By then the supervisor had also observed what guard had indicated. Just few inches near to the feet of the holy shrine, on the temple floor, there were few drops of fresh blood! Both of them were terribly scared. They immediately ran out of the temple and ran towards the Raja's palace to report. They forgot to lock the door.

After much effort they woke up the Raja at midnight and reported the entire incidence. The Raja's sleep being disturbed at such an awkward time of midnight and hearing this kind of story, he became immensely angry and replied that both of them must have been drinking. However, seeing that both the guard and supervisor were convinced, he decided to visit the temple. He took a small troop of soldiers along with him and followed the supervisor and guard towards the temple. When they reached the temple, the temple door was closed and locked as expected. Both guard and supervisor swore that they ran away from the temple and had left the door open and unlocked. The Raja did not believe them and was even angrier. The poor guard and supervisor swore under their breath to have left the temple door open. Anyways, they unlocked the door and went inside the temple to have a look at the shrine. When they reached near to the garbhagriha, everything appeared normal, the holy shrine was properly covered as if never opened and surprisingly enough, there was no blood on the floor!

Raja was furious after this event. He dismissed the supervisor and the guard, next morning and replaced them with a new supervisor and two guards. Although, the Raja made the replacement thinking that the previous supervisor and guard were insane but at the back of his mind he had an uncanny feeling. After all, two people cannot be wrong at the same time. Also, both them confessed to have witness same incidents, there was no difference in their confession. He gave strict instructions to the newly appointed guards and supervisor that this should not be repeated and he must not be disturbed at the mid of night.

That night each guard decided to remain awake in turns and see nothing unwanted happens. Also it was decided that the supervisor would visit once in between to see everything was going well and there was no distraction. Whatever be the arrangement, as the night became darker the guards and the supervisor fell asleep. Towards the mid of night the same strange belly-laughing was heard. The guards became immediately alert and they were terrified. The door was locked as usual and there was no sign of anyone tampering or disturbing the lock. One of the guards called up the new supervisor and all three together went inside. Inside the garbhagriha, they found holy shrine was uncovered and there were drops of blood all over the place, inside and outside the garbhagriha. Also, the holy shrine looked alive. One of the guards fainted and the supervisor fled. The other guard was speechless and remained shocked for a while, then recovered from it slowly and ran towards Raja's palace to report.

Upon patiently listening to the details, the Raja was worried. He immediately summoned a panel of soldiers and marched towards the temple along with his troop led by the guard. Upon reaching the temple, the door was found closed and locked as if no one had opened it. The guard was more scared. He called out the names of other guard and the supervisor but no one responded. They searched for the key to the lock and found it under the supervisor's pillow inside the tent, where it used to be. When they unlocked the door and went inside, they found the other guard lying unconscious on the floor. Raja's troop tried to wake the guard up but he never woke up. The guard had mysteriously died. Worth mentioning, the holy shrine was found properly covered as if it was never opened and there were no drops of blood to be found anywhere. Next, the new supervisor was found unconscious near the river bank. He had high fever and later took significant time to recover from his illness. Also, no body found what had caused the illness.

Raja Samarjit was then truly worried. The news of temple mis-happenings rapidly spread over Arghapur and to nearby towns and villages like a fire outbreak. No purohit was willing to take the job of worshipping the holy shrine, even with lucrative offers. Raja published all over the town and nearby places that high wages and other equivalent remunerations will be given to any purohit who accepts the job. Days went by but no one seemed interested. The inauguration of the holy shrine and worship were indefinitely delayed. Finally one day, a poor purohit showed interest. The purohit was young and in his childhood had lost both of his parents. He was born and brought up by his maternal aunt and gained education and all knowledge regarding puja, rituals and mantras from his uncle. He had a wife but no children.

Raja Samarjit had built a small two roomed hut for his staff little bit away from the temple and closer to the palace. The purohit was offered shelter with his wife at the hut. He had studied his holy books and had suggested Raja Samarjit about a suitable date to inaugurate the temple. The temple was not yet fully bulid but Raja felt if he can initiate worshipping of Goddess Kali as soon as possible then may be her blessings will fall upon everyone and all pending activities will progress smoothly. The purohit had found a new moon day and suggested the Raja that this day was auspicious to inaugurate the temple and commence worshipping of the holy shrine. He had provided the list of materials that will be required for the puja. Raja happily accepted the suggestion.

The temple was inaugurated on the scheduled day, and the rituals related to Goddess Kali's worship proceeded without any hindrance. It was decided that each day the purohit will offer prayer, recite mantras and perform minor rituals while Raja Samarjit will visit the temple on

Tuesdays and Saturdays every week as well as on auspicious days to worship Goddess Kali. On those two days the rituals will be performed in a magnificent way. Raja had appointed the purohit on good salary scale and also a part of puja offerings will be shared with the purohit, while rest will be utilized to purchase puja commodities. Also, from time to time purohit will receive additional benefits. Initially the work progressed smoothly. The villagers were not allowed to worship at the temple and only Raja's family had the privilege of worship.

About one month later, there was another new moon day. The Raja had visited the temple along with his wife, who was then nearing to her expected date, and offered prayers. Raja visited the temple in the morning and had completed the rituals. Towards the mid of night, the temple premises were vacant and only the purohit was available at that time in his hut. The purohit heard a strange noise from his hut which appeared to come from inside the temple. It was not very clear but whatever could be perceived, it appeared as a female laughter. This resulted in a shivering fear to the purohit. The purohit's wife paid a visit to her paternal abode and the purohit was alone in the hut. The purohit walked towards the temple slowly in fear to investigate source of the strange sound. The temple door was closed and locked as expected. He unlocked the gate and entered inside. He had brought a lamp along with him from the hut. He swayed the lamp light inside the temple walls, ceilings and floor but did not find anything unusual. He then approached the garbhagriha to check the holy shrine. From what he saw he screamed in extreme terror. The shrine looked alive and there were drops of blood all over the floor inside the garbhagriha. The eyes of the shrine of Goddess Kali appeared as if they were burning in vengeance. He dropped the lamp on the temple floor in immense fear and immediately ran away from the temple. He hurriedly went towards the Raja's palace. When he was brought in front of the Raja, he was still shivering and gasping for breath. He gave a detailed account of his experience. Raja was then scared and worried. He provided shelter to the purohit in his palace for that night and took a troop of soldiers to survey the temple incidence. Upon reaching the temple he found the temple door was locked as was found in earlier incidents. Raja ordered his soldiers to unlock the temple door. Surprisingly, the temple door's lock took pretty much effort to unlock as if some invisible force was restricting to unlock the door. Even strong arms of the guards were challenged pretty much to unlock.

Inside the temple everything appeared normal as if unexplored. Also, at the garbhagriha there was no drop of blood to be found. However, the shrine of Goddess Kali looked somewhat lively as if very recently it had woken up from sleep. The eyes of the shrine had a burning appearance which was previously never seen. Apart from that nothing unusual was noted. Purohit's encounters had no answers. Raja felt the darkness of the night was causing all those ill thoughts. Raja asked his men to thoroughly check all over inside the temple and garbhagriha but nothing could be discovered. The guards also searched all of the temple premises but nothing unusual was found. Ultimately they gave up, locked the temple door properly and departed from there.

In the morning, Raja summoned the purohit and explained him what they had found last night. The purohit was still confident in what he had observed inside the temple the previous night and stressed upon his experience again and again. After a subtle session of arguments and reasoning, purohit was finally convinced and expressed willingness to get back to work. He agreed that it might have been his mistake in vision, there was actually nothing inside the temple. It must be that he was alone, too scared because of the darkness and due to that he was imagining fancy things. He left the palace and resumed his work from that day. Although the Raja persuaded the purohit, he himself was in great anxiety. By then he believed some demonic shadow had fallen upon the temple and that was not going to stop till everything was ended.

Next few weeks passed by without any event and purohit firmly believed what he saw that night was some kind of temporary hallucination. He was beginning to enjoy his work and had almost forgotten that night's incidents. Raja and his wife used to visit the temple on scheduled days. Since, there was no further ominous event happening, all began to believe that evil days have passed by and splendid days were going to follow. The Rani was nearing to her expected date. The Raja was planning to build the remaining parts of the temple. It was then the most ferocious event occurred. It was one day after another new Moon night. The previous day Raja had visited the temple alone, as Rani was no longer advised to walk outside the palace. The rituals on the previous day went well. At mid-day a villager came running to the palace in extreme fear. He was sick and unable to speak. He barely uttered a few statements and then fainted. From what villager informed all were shocked. From what villager claimed was that his goats were grazing near by the river when one of his goats had moved out of the herd and probably had misled to the direction of the temple. The villager strolled towards the temple in search of his missing goat. When he reached the temple platform he found drops of blood everywhere and was terribly scared. He did not wait to see anything else and immediately came running to the palace to report.

Raja was worried from the villager's description. Raja's soldiers and servants did not feel comfortable either. From the days the sinister events had started happening, one or two of his crew were resigning every now and then and now this news could mean a disaster. The Raja assembled a few soldiers along with him and rushed towards the temple without wasting any time. Upon reaching the temple platform he found that the villager was correct, there were drops of blood everywhere but they were dry due to heat from the Sun. Also, the blood looked fresh. He directed his men to investigate around the temple and also inside to understand the source of this blood. His men found nothing unusual outside the temple. The temple door was half open and inner part of the temple could not be seen. Few men then stepped inside the temple. Almost immediately one of them screamed. Rest of the men and Raja were alarmed and rushed inside the temple to see what the issue was. Near to the garbhagriha was lying a human female corpse with full of fresh blood on the body and all over the place. Upon close observation the corpse was found to be of the temple purohit's wife. There were three deep holes on the throat equidistant from each other. The holes resembled a damage made from a sharp weapon like a Trishul. Raja's guards pointed towards the holy shrine and the Trishul held by the shrine. The sharp edge of the Trishul bearing the three prongs carried dried blood! Purohit was not to be found anywhere. Nothing seemed missing in the purohit's hut except the Purohit. Purohit was searched for days in the village and nearby places as well as in the jungle but never found. It seemed like he had mysteriously disappeared. Since none of the purohit's belongings were found missing, it was assumed that the purohit was dead. However, in reality he was dead or alive still remains a mystery. Lot of efforts was made to resolve the reason behind the brutal killing but no conclusion was reached. Some claimed there was some internal dispute between the couple, that the purohit had murdered his wife with Trishul of the holy shrine, placed it back and fled but this theory did not explain where did the purohit vanish and why no belonging was missing from the hut. Others claimed that this was the curse from the tortured and harassed Pir which brought on this misfortune.

This event led to lot of restrictions. The temple was sealed with immediate effect. The news of this brutal death spread fast and within few days nearby villages and towns came to know about it. The local people were afraid of the place and the temple became infamous as the Cursed Temple. Majority believed it was the curse from the Pir. As the days passed by, the temple premises were abandoned and no one even dared to go near to the temple premises. The Raja faced continued misfortunes and losses in his family business. Majority of the servants and soldiers resigned and went away; only those who were very faithful to the Raja remained. The expected date for Rani was nearing. The first child also mysteriously started suffering from chronic illnesses. Lot of physicians, healers and other healthcare workers both qualified and unqualified were contacted. Some refused to visit the palace, others failed to heal the child and the child remained continuously sick and bedridden.

Raja lost a lot of weight due to anxiety from his continuous damages. He remained silent and lonely most of the time and sometimes accompanied his wife. He also was believed to have secretly made efforts to search for the Pir but it was of no use. He tried astrology, palmistry and other occult art but none came to rescue. On the day the Rani was going to give birth to the second child, it was heavily raining and there were dark clouds all over the sky. The Rani faced great difficulty in giving birth to the second child, lost a lot of blood and was unconscious for a long time after giving birth to the second child. The baby was declared stillborn. However, there were also rumors that Rani gave birth to a deformed male baby. The baby was rumored to be a demon's incarnation with legs of a goat, hairs all over the body, having horns and red eyes but no one knew what happened in reality. The baby was carried away from the palace to an unknown land and was mysteriously hidden or buried, no one knew. Rani was informed that the second child was stillborn.

Few months after these events, Raja left the place with his family and servants and travelled back to north Bengal to his distant relatives and settled there. The first child healed up there with some physical deformities but managed to survive. From last known news, Raja's successors had moved to Calcutta and settled down there. Their broad kingdom no longer exists but a minor fragment is still there somewhere in north Bengal. The palace at Arghapur and the temple were abandoned. With time the palace was dilapidated and turned into ruins while astonishingly the temple survived and retained some luster.

I heard this tale in my childhood. Years turned into decades and decades into centuries, mysteries became mysterious while the temple remained cursed. People talked about the temple, rumor spread like anything and no one even dared to think about the Cursed Temple. Travellers whoever unknowingly went through that place met with ill fate. The temple remained haunted and whoever tried to be courageous or curious, met with mysterious death or some kind of deadly physical damage. You were surprisingly lucky to make it out alive and in one piece. I've not known any man in my life remaining unharmed after visiting the temple premises.

Chapter 10

After telling this story continuously without any break, Hari looked exhausted. I believe this was due to his age. He looked outside the window for a while. I exclaimed, "Can you tell me where can I find the Raja's descendants in Calcutta? I mean do you know the address?"

Hari: "No Sir, I've no idea about this. I infer my landlord might be able to help you with the address. I'll suggest you to forget about this deadly place, go back to your home and never visit this place again".

I said calmly: "I've no such intentions. I do not fear all these rumors. I want to see till end".

Hari tried again sadly: "Please Sir, do not go any further. Call this an end. It has not brought any good till now".

I smiled: "I wish no good for me. I've no family and nothing to lose".

Hari looked at me stupefied, unable to decide what to do. Suddenly he heard someone calling him from the ground floor. He lifted up himself slowly and said, "Your dinner is ready. I'll send my son to fetch it you. Please take rest and forget about the temple". Saying these, he did not wait for my response and quickly departed from the room. He might have thought that I've lost my mind and have become insane.

I moved back on my bed, sat back, resting my spine on a pillow and recollecting and reflecting what Hari had told me. I had some similar experience with the holy shrine of Goddess Kali. Could it be real? I could not ignore the possibility of the realistic view, after all the experience I had encountered. But I want to proceed further; I want to explore the root behind all these rumors or tales, whatever it was. Until I was able to resolve this, it will not bring peace and harmony to my mind and keep disturbing me again and again. I decided to visit the temple again on a New Moon night. Possibly this was near about. Also, I'll need to talk to the landlord to get the present address of the Raja's surviving heirs. After I've gathered these experiences and information,

I can happily go back to my country. I wished no further expeditions in India. Also I planned to write down my experiences that time but unfortunately it had kept pending till date.

Next day in the morning I felt fresh and strong. Quickly I shaved, took a shower and got dressed up in a local attire to visit the town and the landlord's abode. Firstly I visited Mahadeb's shop at the market place. It was bit difficult to find but with Hari's instructions I correctly reached his shop. He owned a fruit shop and also sold few staple foods like potatoes along with fruits. From his shop's appearance it looked like Mahadeb was doing well and didn't have any scarcity of money. I bit my lips with my teeth slightly in deep thought as I felt Mahadeb won't be someone to persuade with money to get information. He looked overwhelmed seeing me at his shop. I had a chit-chat with him and did not ask anything about of the temple, which looked meaningless to me. I then headed towards the landlord's abode in some hope.

Luckily the landlord was at his home at that time. He smiled at seeing me at his door and gave a warm welcome. After some petty exchange of conversations I directly landed on my purpose of visit. He looked solemn at my request. I did not tell him from where I learned the tale behind Arghapur but this was quite evident to him, as I was new at the town and knew only few people.

He slowly replied, "I'll warn you about this temple. I have the current address of Raja's heirs. They have moved to Calcutta but still have a palace and some property somewhere in North Bengal but their chief residence and business dealings are in Calcutta now. Raja had abandoned this place in fear and dismay and never even thought to turn back. He died in North Bengal long time ago. Raja's heirs are descendants of his only son".

I said: "I heard he had another son, who was born deformed".

The landlord was speechless for a moment, then regained his state and replied: "Where did you hear that? It is not true, just a myth. Raja had only one son. Whoever had told this to you, it's a lie".

From his expression the landlord looked like he was quite sure who had given me this information. I still concealed my knowledge session with Hari and said: "I heard a rumor on this. Was not sure whether to believe on this, so asked about it, hoping you can provide some details".

The landlord calmly said: "There are no details. These rumors are rubbish. Raja was survived by only one son, he had no other children".

I shook my head in approval: "I see. May be I heard some false information. Anyways, please provide me the address of the Raja's current heirs' address and that will be helpful to me".

I obtained the address and departed quickly from landlord's abode. It was apparent the landlord was not going to confess or say any word about Raja's second child but I needed to know about this. My next plan was to re-visit the market to make some purchases and to know when the New Moon night was going to arrive. Equipped with all these, I can return to my flat to plan thoroughly what will be my next steps. Obviously I cannot abandon this place and give up the idea to revisit the so called Cursed Temple. After all, although the temple was cursed, harmful or something similar, the shrine was lively, and killed or caused permanent physical damage to all those who visited the temple, it surprisingly did not cause me any harm and this was something which interested me the most.

From the market I came to know two nights away it was a New Moon night. I purchased a light and fine piece of cotton cloth which I can use as a mask against any kind of sedating odour or smoke and a solid wooden staff to use as a protection if required. I also made few enquiries about Arghapur and history behind it to test if the story Hari told me was true. It seemed majority of what Hari told me was true. Some of the Hari's information others could not confirm, it seemed the tale was quite old and the local people had not much knowledge about its happenings. So I had to believe and depend only upon Hari's story. Also, I did not get any clear information about Raja's second child. The information that I obtained on this matter looked more of a rumor and people seemed to have different beliefs but no one gave a sure shot reply. Anyways, after my purchases and enquiries I headed back to my flat to have my lunch and further plans.

In the evening I stayed back at my room and made some quick notes in my little note book regarding my experience at the temple, fragments of information from Hari's tale and what I learned from the local people. A matter looked quite evident. Even though Raja Samarjit might have a second child and hence another inheritor, it was evident that the second child did not receive any share of his estate and property. The current descendants were those from the first child and they inherited all of Raja Samarjit's property or estate, whatever they might be. Also an important question was that if there was in reality any second child, a probable son, then what happened to him? I could not believe that Raja might have put the second child to death just because he was born deformed. Also, was Rani aware about the birth of the second child, deformed? These questions kept on troubling me but I did not find any solution.

Post dinner I chalked out a plan to visit the Cursed Temple on the New Moon night. I hid my belongings that I had purchased in the morning, so that I can easily carry them along with me to the temple. For obvious reasons, I did not inform Hari or anyone about my intentions to revisit the temple. After I revisit the temple and gather adequate evidence, I'll return to Calcutta. In Calcutta my exploration on this mystery will be pursued further by contacting the Raja's current heirs. I was not sure how to approach them or what reason behind my visit I should tell them. Obviously I cannot give them the true story about my visit to Arghapur and the Cursed Temple. May be I can present myself as an author and an explorer who was looking out for just a decent story, possibly that might help. Anyways, I kept those thoughts aside for now and laid focus on my current plans. After that I went to the bed quickly and quickly fell asleep.

Chapter 11

Finally, the New Moon night has arrived! Tonight was the time for which I had patiently waited. I had planned to visit the temple after dark at around midnight, when Hari and his family would be asleep and the whole town will be silent. I had lied to Hari that at night I want to take a walk outside the house, to the market and back to home. Initially he objected to my idea but somehow I convinced him to believe that if I have to write about this town and the tale in which Hari and his contribution will also be included, then I need to remain awake and stroll through the town to enhance my thought process. This will in fact boost my thinking like an author.

I had prepared myself for this night. After dinner I slept briefly and woke up before midnight. I took the piece of cloth which I had purchased from a shop in the market. I wrapped a blanket around me and took the wooden staff and torch. I silently locked my flat and quietly left the house without waking up anyone. I directly went to the river and started walking slowly towards the temple. It was new moon night and so there was no support of moon light. The path from the village's end towards the river was illuminated poorly by the faint beam of light that radiated from the last village huts. The jungle on the other side of the river appeared darker. I had to use the torch as the faint light was not at all sufficient to guide my path towards the temple. The river bank which had appeared clear and soothing the other day I had visited this place, now looked mysterious and scary. The night was cool and calm with no sign of life.

As the temple approached nearer and nearer, my heart beat pounded rapidly. I can feel a cold scary chilling sensation running down my spine. Once or twice from the distant wood I heard some nocturnal bird, possibly it was an owl or something similar. I had no experience with birds, so I could not make out.

When I was within a stone throwing distance from the temple, I noticed a beam of light to come from inside the temple that had illuminated a portion of the temple and the platform on which the temple stood. The temple's rear portion faced the river bank and so the front part was not visible from where I approached the temple. However, due to night being dark, one can easily make out light coming out from inside the temple. I felt shivering and was terribly scared. I switched off my torch light and stood motionless for a while. I needed to make a decision whether to proceed ahead. The tale behind the temple and the curse had left a shocking and terrorizing sensation in my heart. However, I was not willing to give up and was rather desperate, despite the scary tale I had learned. After all, I had nothing to lose! Finally I made up my mind to see through the end.

I had put some water on the cloth, not wetting it completely, that I had brought along with me and wrapped it around my face tightly. This will protect me from any obnoxious sedating odour hopefully. The way the odour drugged me last time and I could not make out the smell, I decided not to take any risk tonight. I need to remain awake and not fall asleep. The water I poured over the cloth might act as a temporary shield by absorbing some part of the harmful chemicals in the odour or smoke, whatever it was.

I then slowly, silently and patiently moved towards the temple platform. I climbed up the steps without making any noise and came in front of the temple. As expected from distance, a strong beam of light came from inside the temple and illuminated the entire temple platform. I looked all around the temple premises but could see no one. I also felt that strange sedating smell like last time. However, the cloth served as protective mask to filter the bad effects. I hold the wooden staff I my right hand firmly and slowly moved towards inside of the temple.

Inside the temple, strong rays of light appeared to be coming from inside the garbhagriha. I could not locate any sign of life inside the temple from outside but heard two voices coming from inside the garbhagriha where the holy shrine was placed. One was a harsh male note and another female laughter. The female voice resembled belly-laughing! I was dead cold by now. I remained in trance for a while, then regained consciousness and moved towards the garbhagriha to have a closer look on the owners of the two peculiar scary voices.

As I reached at the entrance of garbhagriha, I came across the worst experience of my life. An experience I cannot express in words. I was shocked, horribly scared and unable to move, as if I was frozen into a statue. I tried to speak but could not utter a word. I was unsure how was I still standing and conscious. Inside the garbhagriha the holy shrine of Goddess Kali was alive, eyes were red and burning, the trishul was lifted up and held in both hands and drops of blood were all over the place. Worse than that an inhuman, abominable creature was standing at a few feet distance from the shrine and worshipping or something like that, with blood in a human skull in one hand and some smoky incense sticks in the other. The creature had a harsh growling voice like some wild beast, it had red and black hairs all over the body and its legs resembled that of a goat. Resting on the wall by the right side of the shrine was a kharag, an Indian sword which is twisted towards it edge which resembles a crescent. This is a weapon of Goddess Kali and is used to slice off the head of sacrifice offered to the Goddess.

Suddenly the beast turned towards me and exclaimed in a growling voice. The language was Bengali! He pointed towards me and said, "Ma Kali is thirsty. Ma wants blood, fresh human blood! I'll sacrifice you to satisfy her thirst". I could not stare at the creature's face as it was not human, I cannot describe what it looked like. I can only remember the creature's eyes were red and those hypnotized me to come close to the shrine. I tried to slightly bend down my head and immediately looked away from the creature.

With full strength I tried to remain conscious. I turned back quickly and took first step to run. Strange! The beast had changed its place and was standing at the entrance door and blocking it. I turned back to the shrine and found beast was not there and the trishul had vanished from the hand of the shrine of Goddess Kali. More strangely, the peculiar sedating odour was intensified and all over the air. Although I covered my nose with the wet cloth, still I can feel the intensity of the odour. The moist mask was barely capable to form a barrier for the odour. The odour was drugging me and I was gradually set to lose my consciousness. I then heard a sweet female voice from outside the temple entrance. This was the same voice which I had heard previously. I was unable to make out what were the words. However, it was apparent that it was something related to me. From the flash of light I observed a feminine figure to move inside the temple. The female figure was wearing a white saree with red border and was covered from head to toe in that saree. I could not see the face or hands. After a bit of conversation between the beast and the female, I suddenly found the beast to become harsh and went on to attack the female. Probably the feminine figure was trying to protect me and the beast denied the same.

Instantaneously, I felt a bit angry, charged up and felt to protect the female. I held the staff in my hand and with full strength rushed towards the beast and with greater strength targeted the portion of its skull just above the right ear, since skull is thin at this place. I heard an intense thudding sound and without second thought I tried to give another blow. After the second blow I felt feeble and was barely able to stand on my feet. I tried to look towards the shrine to locate if the trishul was there which I could use at this time but could not find it. I dropped on my feet, breathing heavily. I saw the beast advancing towards me at an astonishing speed. I thought this was my end. When the beast was within few inches from me, I was surprised to see the trishul in the hands of the feminine figure. I could not see her visage. Possibly she had picked it up when I was hitting the beast and subsequently fell down on my feet. With full strength I tried to stand up on my feet but did not feel any strength in my legs. The hairy beast was filled with inhuman laughter, laughter echoed from the temple walls. The last scene that I saw or could remember was that the feminine figure trying to resist the beast from approaching towards me with the trishul. I then dropped off on the ground on my right side and lost consciousness.

Chapter 12

Strong Sun's rays flooded my room and bothered my eyes. I heard some voices too and slowly opened my eyes. Someone immediately muttered, "Babu is awake. Thank God he is okay!"

I was still dizzy but could make out that I was in a room. Gradually I regained consciousness and realized I was on my bed in my room. The speaker was undoubtedly Hari. There was one unknown face in the room along with Hari and the landlord. From the appearance of the stranger he looked like a local doctor or a medic. I had fully regained consciousness by then. I was unsure how long I'd been asleep. From the strong sunlight it looked like midday. I tried to lift up myself on my bed but felt little bit feeble and dizzy. The drug effect still did not go away. I rested myself in a slanting position and supported my neck with the pillow. This gave me somewhat relaxation and swapped away my dizziness to some extent. I looked at the three people in the room one by one. The doctor felt my pulse, examined my eyes, nose, ears and tongue. He then checked my skull and hands. He asked, "Do you feel pain in any part of your body."

I mildly replied, "No I'm fine but little dizzy."

Doctor: "Any injury or damages?"

I replied in same tone, "I'm fine, I've no injury."

The doctor said, "You were found lying unconscious at the temple steps today morning. Can you recall how you reached there? Can you tell us what happened to you?"

I said, "I'm not sure how I reached the temple steps. I decided to take short by the side of the river bank after my dinner. I did not go near to the temple." I wondered how I reached there. I clearly remembered to fall down inside the temple near to the garbhagriha but I cannot reveal this to these people.

The doctor asked, "Could you remember how you lost your consciousness? I'm implying that if there is no injury in any part of your body as you claimed then what is the cause of your unconsciousness?"

I replied: "Not sure. I felt the smell of some strange odour in air and it caused me immense drowsiness. Possibly after that I fell down and lost consciousness."

The doctor looked thoughtful for a moment and then looked at landlord and said, "Nothing serious. He does not seem to have any kind of injury. Though true cause of unconsciousness is strangely inconclusive."

I questioned to Hari, "How long I've been asleep? How did I come here?"

Hari: "Babu in the morning we did not find you in your room, we became worried. I gathered two local villagers and Mahadeb, me and the two local residents started looking for you. After much searching we found you near the temple staircases. Babu after so much warning you did not listen to us. Thanks to Goddess Kali that you are still alive and unharmed."

I replied, "You are mistaken I did not intentionally go towards the temple. I was walking beside the river for fresh air and planned to return home after half an hour of stroll. I'm unsure how I was misdirected and went to the temple steps." I lied and completely concealed the happenings of last night.

The landlord looked thoughtfully at me, clearly revealing he did not believe in me. He spoke now, "With God's grace you are safe now. Please do not go near to the river bank again. You must leave this place as early as possible so that no unearthly events happen. You can take it as our humble and earnest request. I'm sorry to put it this way but please try to understand our situation and consider our request. If anything happens to you, we'll be questionable and face great danger from the British government."

The landlord looked serious and not in a mood of joking. So this will be the end. I've to depart without any evidence and inconclusive result. Ultimately, mysteries will remain as mysterious. I looked outside the window and sighed. There was no way out. The local people will not allow me to go any further, this was the end. I can understand their point of view. So what now? I felt tremendous uneasiness due to the idea of abandoning this place. I replied briskly, "Okay, I understand you. I'll leave this place tomorrow morning. Is it possible for you to arrange for a palki?"

The landlord looked glad now and replied, "I'll make all the arrangements. You need not worry. Please rest today and pack your belongings. We'll also pack you some local artwork so that you can remember this place." And this was true, I did not forget them till today.

Once everyone left the room, I went to the washroom and washed my face with cold water. I felt refreshed, this was prime requirement at this moment. It was already afternoon and I've been unconscious from midnight. I've no choice left but to leave this place. The last night's encounter was terrible but I cannot speak about it to anyone, no one will believe. The incidents of last night had left me in a partial shock. I was glad that I'm still alive and surprised at the same time. Also, there was no injury and no pain. Could it be the drug's effect? Hopefully not as I'm fully conscious now which indicates drug effect is no longer available.

While I was deeply immersed in such thoughts, Hari came into the room with a bowl of soup and some snacks in a tray. He said, "Babu, please have some food. The doctor advised to feed you with some some soft and easily digestible food." He put down the bowl and the tray on the table and looked at me in a peculiar way.

I asked, "Is there anything you want to tell me?"

Hari: "It's unfortunate that you have to leave this place. Hope we've served you well."

I replied: "Your service was exceptional. I'll remember for the rest of my life."

Hari: "Thank you Babu. I'll remember you too! You were so friendly and down to Earth! For one moment I never felt you are from a foreign land. Please rest today Babu, I'll pack some food and artwork for your tomorrow's journey. Our landlord will bring back some artwork in short while."

He hesitantly stood there for a while as if he wanted to say something else. I asked, "What is it? You can tell me without any hesitation."

Hari: "Babu, the temple is evil but it causes no harm to people with pure in heart. You are a good soul and so it did not harm you."

I: "If that's so, then how come during Raja Samarjit's time, the purohit and his wife, as per your story, received curse of the temple and were killed or lost, whatever it was?"

Hari: "The purohit and his wife were not pure in their heart. There were rumors that they were thieves and used to steal from temple stores and jewellery, wherever they were hired. The temple will not hurt anyone who is wise and has pure soul. Raja Samarjit was no good either, he caused lot of mischiefs to many people. He was greedy and did not care for common people of his kingdom."

It gave a plausible explanation of why I'm still alive. But what about the monster which I saw inside the temple last night? Was it a human? Was it the younger son of Raja Samarjit who was probably taken away and hid somewhere? Even if I assume that the temple monster was Raja Samarjit's younger son, then this son cannot be alive, the events Hari described, happened at least more than one hundred years ago. Which raises concern that the temple inhabitants last night, were they alive or dead? Whatever it was, one thing was clear to me; the female figure tried to protect me. Who was she?

Suddenly something crossed my mind. I asked Hari, "Do you know Christopher?"

Hari: "Chis, who?"

I: "Did any British traveller previously visit this place?"

Hari's face enlightened. "Yes Babu. Few years back there was an English Babu, who came to this place for collecting artwork. He stayed in this town somewhere in a cottage for few days and then left. He was very kind to all the people. He stayed near to the market. I do not know his name."

I: "Did he visit the temple?"

Hari strongly shook his head and said, "No no Babu, no as far as I know."

There was some food on the table, possibly Hari has brought my lunch. I abruptly became quite and looked blankly at the food lying on the table. Seeing me quite and staring at the meal, Hari possibly thought I was hungry and tired and so without any further discussion left the room. After deep thinking I finally decided to find out the address and visit the Raja's current descendants. Probably they might have the answers to my questions. I now firmly believe that spirits or ghosts whatever they might be, are for real. I've no other choice left. My expedition ends here but before leaving I'll definitely visit the temple one last time and that has to be immediately post-lunch. Possibly after finding few answers to my questions, I'll return to my homeland. The events are going to haunt me for long time.

I hurriedly had my lunch and put on some fresh clothes and left the room silently. I rushed towards the temple with the expectation to find few answers and for my last visit. Upon reaching the temple premises, as usual it was empty. The temple premises looked more shabby and dirty compared to what it appeared in the evening. The intact panel of the door was closed and appeared like it had not been opened for a long time. I went inside the temple through the dilapidated portion. Inside the temple was in a worse condition compared to outside. Climbers have invaded the inside the temple and grown through the walls which were full of cracks and fissures. I quickly moved towards the shrine.

The shrine of Goddess Kali stood quiet and still in front of me as if it was always dead like this. The picture was uninteresting, however, the eyes of the shrine still looked bright. I was disappointed at this scene. I looked all through the temple thoroughly in search of something interesting but was further disappointed. The atmosphere inside the temple was normal like an old place and I did not smell the strange odour. I left the temple and headed back towards my room.

Chapter 13

An old servant guided me to a drawing room inside the well-furnished house. While passing through the corridor I felt the house was more like a palace rather than a common man's abode. Raja's descendants have made quite a progress in their lives. I passed by several rooms before I reached the drawing room. The drawing room was more like a hall. The drawing room was furnished with expensive wooden furniture; I could smell the odour of teakwood, cedar, sandal, etc. There were several paintings all over the walls depicting family history. As I had previously not seen any of Raja Samarjit's pictures, I could not make out him from the picture. Near to the north-east corner of the drawing room there was a wooden almirah with glass door. From a glance it revealed several collections of old books and possibly manuscripts or something similar. The glass door was locked.

I had returned to Calcutta 2 days ago and it costed me some efforts to find Raja's current descendants. I had made several inquiries over these past 2 days. Also, I visited the National Library and several other book stalls to find books on Arghapur but I was disappointed each time. It seems this was not yet revealed to the mankind. Possibly the rumors were not allowed to spread and secrets remained buried within Raja's family. The journey back to Calcutta was uneventful. The people at Arghapur had shown great love and respect and while departing I felt flattered and truly disappointed. I had never imagined that the journey will end in this way. The night before departing I could not sleep well and the temple events kept on troubling me. May be I'll never again find peace in my life and these events will become nightmare. I was not good at praying but the events brought some changes in me. I prayed to God and requested for solace from then on. I could not forget the horrible sight of that night and the beast.

After waiting for around half an hour, I was attended by a servant and served with a glass of lemonade or something like that. When I asked what that was, the servant replied, "Sherbat, with honey." After I took my first sip, it felt something like a heavenly drink. While I was enjoying the Sherbat, a man aged in early thirties came into the room. He was wearing white kurta and pajama. From his appearance he looked somewhat similar to one of the paintings. I guessed he was probably Raja Samarjit's inheritor.

The man introduced himself as Rudranath Roy. I falsely introduced myself as an art enthusiast and an author and explained my purpose of visit was to know about the family history of Raja Samarjit Roy. Rudranath informed that he was the great grandson of Raja Samarjit. His younger brother and he were descendants of Raja Samarjit and the only successors alive apart from their father. His younger brother has went abroad to study law and that Rudranath looks after the entire current property or whatever was left of it.

I asked, "I travel a lot. I travelled throughout India and came to Calcutta few days ago. I happened to be at Bolpur for few days to visit Shantiniketan. It was in Bolpur that I came to know your ancestors were once kings and ruled at northern parts of Bengal. So when did you leave northern part of Bengal?"

Rudranath: "This happened during my father's generation. My father sold majority of the property in north Bengal and settled down in Calcutta. He started a garment business and established himself in the same. I look after the business now as my father has been bedridden for two years."

I did not waste words and directly jumped into the topic. I said, "I'm exploring the history of your great grandfather. I'm planning to write a book on artwork and include the history. At Bolpur I came to know about Arghapur and the kind of artwork it had to offer. Based on what I learned, I had taken a trip to Arghapur few days before to collect some artwork. At Arghapur I came to know about a tale behind the Cursed Temple and your ancestors being involved in the same. Could you please give some lead on it?"

Rudranath looked dismayed and remained quiet for a moment. He then came back in a confident tone, "There is no tale, no Cursed Temple. The tale was developed by the villagers for amusement and as bed time stories to frighten the children. My great grandfather at one point in his life realized that there is no future in that small town and so moved out."

I realized Rudranath was not going to reveal the secrets and there was no point in arguing for same. I had no proof. As claimed by Rudranath, the story behind the Cursed Temple was in fact delivered to me by Hari, who is a villager. Had it not been the sequence of horribly scary events I encountered, I might not have believed in Hari. I asked, "Oh, I see. Never mind. I just heard some rumors from villagers. Can you help me with any manuscript or writing about Raja Samarjit from which I can learn some more about his kingdom and rule? I looked around for books but found none."

Rudranath looked reluctant and showed no interest, "There is nothing special. Raja Samarjit lead a normal life and towards the end of his life decided to move out of that meager place, in search of better future."

I felt it is required to provide some inducement to make this interesting. I said, "Well I was planning to include his rule and kingdom in my book. If you could help me, I'll put your name under the chief contributors who helped me to write this book. The book will be published in England and I'll send a copy of it to you."

This sounded something interesting to him. From his tone he seemed flattered. "Well that's great. I'll see what I can do for it. I personally do not have much idea. There is an old box full of papers down in the stack room which belonged to Raja Samarjit. I'll ask one of my servants to bring it up to you. You can take the box with you and return it when you are finished. There is no hurry. Please take your own time."

So I got the bull's eye. Now I've to wait to see what the box has to offer. I asked, "What's there in the box?"

Rudranath: "Some old papers, not related anything to property or of commercial value. We never read those. The box had been kept aside for several decades. No one ever felt interested to go through them."

I felt a bit disheartened. If I had to evidence the incidents then some books or old paperwork on Raja Samarjit's history could be useful. From my exploration, I did not find anything suggesting the history. This box was my last hope. If there had been some secret concealed from the world, then there should be some documentation of that. Since Rudranath claimed no one was interested in the paperwork held within the box, it seemed quite obvious the papers were of no use. However, there still might be some hope. May be people have missed or ignored some subtle information held within the box.

I asked, "Can I keep the box with me for a day or do?"

Rudranath looked elated: "Of course! If you require, you can even go ahead and keep it with you for one week or more. The box is lying down at the stack room and dirty. I'll ask one of servants to clean it up and bring it to you." He summoned one of his servants and immediately ordered to bring up the box and also instructed to thoroughly clean it up before delivering it to me.

He then turned at me, "You'll need to excuse me now. I've some pre-occupied engagements and will need to leave now. The box will be with you in no time. If you require anything else, you can ask my servant." With this he ended the conversation and shortly after left the room.

Few minutes later, an old servant brought me an old wooden box, size of a small luggage box. The box was made of mahogany or some similar wood. It was square in shape and blackish brown in color. Probably with age the wood had darkened, however it was still in great shape. From the size of the box I could make out there was not much inside it and I can easily carry it to my small flat. I collected the box, thanked the servant and then headed towards the street. I was excited and could not wait to see what was inside the box.

Chapter 14

It had been over 1 month that I did not practice medicine. My expedition had badly impact my medical knowledge and throughout my stay in India I never had a chance to utilize my skills in medicine. After that severe incident, I had decided to call my expedition a standstill, at least for a while. When I'll return to my home country, I'll resume my profession and will not think about anything else at least for some time.

It was end of February and already the climate was turning warm. From the wooden box I had obtained from Rudranath's abode, I extracted quite few details with much difficulty. Majority of the text written on the papers had almost volatilized due to age and the papers were in terrible condition due to lack of maintenance. Lot of pages was also missing. This was the best I could get and there was no further hope. I deciphered the writings and noted them down over several pages in my notebook. Then I edited the same to remove unwanted texts and kept only the important ones.

There was a brief episode of rain earlier this morning and showers of rain brought some relief to warm weather. I had barely gone out of my room for last 2 days, only reading and deciphering the work that came in the wooden box. A lot of details and mysteries still remain unexplained and probably will remain concealed forever. However, from what I could extract and collect in a note book explained few things. I'm trying to put story from Raja Samarjit's point of view.

Last Words from Raja Samarjit

I, Raja Samarjit Roy, spending last few days of my life, am trying to reveal few secrets which I've kept hidden from the world till date. These secrets were not even known to my wife till her last day. I'm suffering from tuberculosis and doctors have tried all possible medications but none were successful. I hardly have few more weeks or even less. I'll store these in my wooden box, the only property I have as of now to my knowledge.

When human beings attain power and money, they become blind with conceit. They consider them as no less than the almighty, perform most treacherous and disgraceful acts on other human beings, taking advantage of their poverty and weakness and make them suffer; they ignore what God has created, and then God's curse fall upon them. In my youth I've performed such treacherous activities that I cannot explain and yet did not realize for a moment. My actions did not satisfy my thirst and they became worse day by day. My parents were unhappy to see their child being wasted and thought after marriage I'll improve but nothing worked out. As I became older, I became crueler. I gave values to only those who were my devoted to me and worked for me with extreme obsequiousness. As a result I forgot humanity, overlooked the poor and honest people and went on doing whatever I wished. I put lot of thieves to death mercilessly for petty issues, disregarded pious and holy people and lot others which cannot be described. Being a king, it was my duty to see that my kingdom and people residing in it were happy and satisfied but I ignored my righteous duties. I over taxed the poor farmers, I forced them to pay and if they couldn't, my men would torture them, snatch their all belongings, sometimes forcing them to abandon their lands and chase them out of the village.

However, every negative activity has a negative consequence and one day or the other will return to us. The day my men tortured and chased away the Pir from my temple, I should've arrested the barbarian act and instead provided shelter to that poor Pir. The poor Pir was seeking only a shelter for some time and as Raja I should have satisfied his requirement. When he cursed, I laughed at him and ignored him. My blinding over conceit blurred my thoughts and kept me away from thinking what was right and what was logical. I ignored Pir's curse and it destroyed my life, my family and my business. I appointed the young purohit and his wife at my temple to worship goddess Kali, regardless of knowing their ill deeds from past and warnings from my near and dear ones.

The day my wife bore me a male child, I was extremely happy. I spent lots of money after my child's birth. I was over conceited that money can buy everything. Cruelty and greediness had blinded me. Alas! It was too late to understand morals and values of life and humanity. There was no scope left to replenish all that I've destroyed.

It was rainy season when my wife gave birth to second child. On the day my second child was born, it was raining heavily, there were dark clouds in the sky with frequent lightening. These were indicative of a premonition that a demon was approaching. My wife suffered from severe painful condition, bleede heavily, remained sick and tired for the entire day and almost at mid night gave birth to my second child. When my second child was born, my wife was fortunately in an unconscious state and did not realize what was happening. There were only few trustworthy maids in the room and my wife was attended by an old midwife.

At midnight when the baby was born, at the first sight of the baby midwife fainted in extreme fear, same happened to few other maids as well. One of the maids regained consciousness and informed me of the child. I hurriedly reached the room where my wife was still lying unconscious on the bed. The child was wrapped in a warm cloth and placed in a separate small cot. The midwife had recovered by then. I removed the warm cloth from the child's body and witnessed the most horrible scene of my life. A demon in a human body! The baby had reddish brown hairs all over its body, its eyes appeared red and I could not look into them. The legs resembled a goat. I immediately fell down in shock. After a while I recovered and looked at the abominable creature again.

The creature smiled at me. There was something in its smile. It hypnotized me, I could not think for a while. I strolled in great anxiety all around the room and patiently waited for my wife to regain consciousness. Initially I was in the opinion to show the baby to my wife, wait for her reaction and then take it away and put to death. But then, I had dilemma. What if my wife disapproves this idea? What if she wants the baby? Even worse, she might not be able to accept the truth, she might be in shock or the situation can lead to severe damage. After lot of arguments going through in my mind I finally decided to drive the baby away from the palace and put it to death, without my knowing about it. The maids and midwife being loyal to me were trustworthy. There were only 3 maids and the midwife in the room and I could easily get their assurance never to reveal the truth, I'll bribe them for keeping this a secret. The incidents from birth to death of this child or more precisely this demonic creature will remain hidden from the world and everyone will come to know that my wife had a stillbirth. The only barrier could be my wife, whom I loved most. Once she comes to know that she had given birth to a dead child, she won't be able to accept this. She might enter into a trauma, she might faint or even worse. I had to console her somehow and make her belief of the stillbirth.

I decided that I myself would drive the baby away from the palace and put it to death and take help of no one. I requested the midwife to administer some sedative to the baby, so that it remains asleep and silent. After I ensured that the baby was asleep, I silently left the palace through the back door, in my horse. The maids have wrapped the baby in warm clothes and put it in a box. The box was used as a precaution so that no one could make out what was in it. It was the size of luggage box, square-shaped, brown color and made out of mahogany. The night was dark and there was still lot of time for sunrise. I also had carried a shovel and a lantern with me. Due to clouds the Moon was hidden and I had to depend on the faint beam of light from the lantern which showed me the path through the wood. I rode steadily on my horse through the wood. The idea was to find a suitable place in the middle of the wood where it was dense and bury the box and thus the baby in it.

After riding for about half an hour, I reached the middle of the wood. I found the plantation over there quite dense and the place was not inhabited by humans. I found a small piece of land suitable for the burial. I dug deep inside the earth. I was then ready to bury the box. Just before I was ready to bury, I had a thought to open the lid and take look at the baby. I'm not sure why this thought came to my mind. This idea to look inside the box proved disastrous. I found the baby was awake. As I looked inside the box, my eyes met with those of the baby's. The baby smiled at me and its red eyes again hypnotized me. I stood dazzled for a while and unable to react. Whatever happened to me at that moment, I was unsure of it. I felt as if the baby had assumed a human form and is persuading me not to bury it. I could not bury the baby. Instead of burying, I took the box including the baby with me and rode out of the wood on my horse. Outside the wood I searched for a locality and came across a small temple. For one last time I looked at the creature in my arms. I then left the baby wrapped in warm clothes outside the temple door and took the box with me. I returned to the palace with the box and placed it under my cot. I could not sleep for rest of the night.

In the morning, a servant informed that my wife was conscious again but no one revealed that she had a stillbirth. She was searching for her baby and repeatedly asking where it was kept. When the servant asked if they will reveal it to her wife that the baby was dead, I softly and dryly replied "No". Whatever happened I had to face this.

I found only this much from the Raja Samarjit's writings and then there were missing pages and thus information contained in them was missing too. I found few more pages which mentioned that Raja Samarjit had searched for the baby later on in the morning but did not find it. I cannot imagine what might have happened to the baby and baby's mother. However, the creature I saw that night in the Cursed Temple had definitely much resemblance to this baby or probably the baby had grown up to live. Whatever or whoever it might be, one thing for sure the creature cannot be alive. Raja Samarjit's wife gave birth to that creature more than one hundred years ago and no human, although the term "human" is not fit for it, can live that long. A conundrum remains! I looked at that box carefully. It matched the description in Raja Samarjit's writings, except for the color, which has darkened over the ages. This is possibly the box which was used to carry the baby away from the palace or possibly not. Who knows about these? I sat back on my bed for a while trying to find and tie up the missing strings to get into a more plausible conclusion. After 2 days of tirelessly research and logical thinking, I arrived at almost nothing, except that there was another living heir to Raja Samarjit but no one can prove it. So this was the end and I had to return to my home. Good thing about all these was that I was still alive and unharmed. Anyways, before I departed for London, I need to visit my old friend Christopher and say goodbye to him. Tomorrow after returning the box, I'll visit Christopher's home.

Chapter 15

I was bit melancholy to return the wooden box to Rudranath. Rudranath looked elated to see me. He wanted to know if my research was successful and my goal was accomplished. I could not tell him the truth, instead I informed whatever Rudranath told me earlier was true and the box seemed to be a piece of garbage. Rudranath humbly requested me that whatever I had learned about their family history from the local people of Arghapur, to keep them discreet as far as possible. He was worried that a revelation of this kind might be disastrous to their ages old family reputation and that in turn might be harmful to their family business. I assured him the same, exchanged warm handshakes and said goodbye.

My next stop was Christopher's abode. I travelled towards the southern part of Calcutta where he lived. Although I did not possess the card that carried his home address but from the memory of my last visit to his abode, I was confident that I will easily locate his home. Near to midday I reached the area where he lived. I passed by the pond and the group of coconut trees. I remembered that this was the same pond and the same coconut trees which I had passed by, the evening when I visited Christopher's home for the first time. After passing the pond and walking for a while, I came across few houses which looked newly built. From my previous visit I could recall that there was hardly any house within one mile of Christopher's home. I stood under a tree and wondered for a while if I was heading towards a wrong direction.

I again returned to the pond and restarted. This time I fixed my direction towards Christopher's home and walked towards it. I again came across those new houses. This time I decided to go pass through them and travel further. After walking for some time I came across a lonely place. Possibly I have hit the right direction this time. The newly built houses which I had passed by few minutes ago puzzled me. I could clearly remember from my last visit that there was no house nearby. From where those few houses originated in such a short duration between my visits, I could not explain myself. I tried to arrive at some simple explanation and convinced myself by stating that may be last time when I had visited this place, I possibly might have missed to see those new houses because of the darkness.

Travelling further like this, few minutes later, I arrived at the front of an old dilapidated house. It startled me! The house had a broken-down iron gate with very less engravings made from brass. The right portion of the gate was totally demolished and cleared the entrance towards the house. The left part of the gate appeared weak, full of rust and climber plants unevenly grew throughout the iron bars of the remaining portion and almost covered it. I was not prepared for this scene. The scene caused a twist in my mind and left me dazed for a while. When I regained senses, I found I had crossed the broken gate and was standing beside the small garden. The garden looked messed up. It was covered with small shrubs, spider webs and ants which gave a dirty appearance. I could not think what should be my next course of action. This cannot be Christopher's house which I had visited previously but my surroundings clearly told me by every means that I had come to the right house. I went passed the garden and came to the front of the house, dilapidated of course and even worse condition than the surrounding. I remained dazed for a while again. I then called out Christopher's name in low voice twice, waited for a while and then shouted. After shouting few times, I heard a voice from behind.

"Babu, why are you shouting? Are you looking for someone? No one lives here."

The owner of the voice was an old aged man, looked like some kind of labor, more like a gardener. He had white beard which travelled almost towards the temples of his head. His face was almost hidden from his beard. There were wrinkles below his eyes from old age and cheeks were sunk-in. I turned towards this newly appeared stranger and faced him directly.

I replied to him in Bengali, "I'm looking for a friend. His name is Christopher."

I then paused a little and changed my mind to hide some relevant details before proceeding further. I told him, "I was informed that my friend lives here."

The gardener looked surprised and said, "Are you sure Babu? No one has lived in this house for several years."

This time I replied, "Yes I'm sure, this is the house."

The gardener strangely looked at me and was speechless. I realized what mistake I had made. To correct myself I asked, "May be I'm at the wrong address by mistake. Can you tell me if you know someone with the name Christopher Davis who lives in this part of Calcutta?"

The gardener said, "Not sure about any name Babu. There was one British Sahib who purchased some land and built this house over here, quite few years ago. The Sahib was short heighted, bald headed and little bit obese. He and his wife used to reside here. Both Sahib and Memsahib were very kind. I worked in their garden, used to maintain and water all the plants and flower pots inside their house. They had two daughters, both of whom live abroad. The daughters used to visit once or twice in a year".

This was another of my wild experiences. This was undoubtedly the man I had known for a last few weeks, who had been so kind to me and gave a direction to my life's path and to the intentions with which I had come to India.

The old gardener coughed a little, he looked feeble with age. He took a deep breath, shook his head and then continued, "Unfortunately few years ago, may be 5 or 6 years, I clearly do not remember, Babu fell sick and that sickness caused his end".

I could not believe in my ears! This was something breathtaking for me! I asked, "What did you say, his end?"

The gardener looked at me in a melancholic way, "Yes Babu. 5 or 6 years ago, Sahib returned home with high fever and weakness. Local doctor diagnosed him of suffering from severe malaria. More experienced doctor was summoned up from the city but before that doctor could come up, he died."

I stood there motionless. I was like moonstruck. I wondered what was happening. How could it be possible? The man I met few weeks ago, with whom I chatted, laughed and exchanged thoughts, was already dead! Or rather I had spent time with some ghost!

The gardener continued in his own tone, "After Sahib expired, Memsahib could not bear the pain. She remained unhappy all the time and did not eat properly. Day by day she became weak and started suffering from chronic deficiency disorders. She also started consuming excessive alcohol at the same time. She often claimed that she heard her husband's voice, could see him and he used to speak to her. Few months later Memsahib fell sick. The daughters were informed by Sahib's local family doctor about their mother's illness. Memsahib could not make it. By the time the daughters reached the home, Memsahib had already expired. I stayed till Memsahib's funeral and post that left this place."

I felt hysterical. I could hardly believe in my ears. This was the worst thing that could have happened. I took out my handkerchief and buried down my lips under my handkerchief. I stood motionless for a while. I asked, "What happened after that?"

The gardener said, "The house was left barren after this. All expensive wall hangings and furniture were sold out and few were taken away by the daughters. The house is on sale from a long time but no one had turned up yet. Recently someone had shown interest to buy this, as far I as I know". He looked at me suspiciously and questioned, "Who gave you this address?"

I ignored his question and asked, "Where can I find the local doctor who treated the owner of this house?"

The gardener replied, "He lives nearby. I don't know his address but can guide you to his home."

I said, "This sounds good."

I followed the directions of the old gardener and reached the doctor's home within half an hour. I introduced myself to the doctor and informed him that I heard about this vacant house and expressed interested to purchase it. I told him that I wanted to know the detailed history behind this house before I could proceed to purchase it. The doctor gave me the same story as the old gardener, except that he mentioned owner's name as Christopher and Martha as his wife. This removed my further suspicions, if any were still remaining. I could not believe in my ears. For a single moment I did not have any suspicion about Christopher or his wife. Also, I was surprised as why Christopher had lied to me that he had recovered from malaria and returned home healthy. Did Christopher or rather his spirit have intentionally illustrated me the tale of Cursed temple, or rather the tale was altogether near to be true!

Who was the person I had met in the club that evening and who were the residents at Christopher's abode with whom I had dinner the other evening? These unanswered questions still remain a challenge and an enigmatic debate to me. I hunted down through my mysterious experiences uncountable times in search of a plausible justification from the time of my visit to Calcutta to my encounter with the demon at the temple and then this Christopher's tale, painfully and incredulously thought about them again and again and every time came up with unexplained and non-semantic answers. These enigmatic experiences have tormented my mind and haunted my dreams for several nights and undoubtedly will do so for the rest of my life.

The End

www.ingramcontent.com/pod-product-compliance
Lightning Source LLC
Chambersburg PA
CBHW061332140726

47997CB00003B/953